DEATH WORE A SMART LITTLE OUTFIT

Orland Outland

BERKLEY PRIME CRIME, NEW YORK

For my mother
We lived to see the day

DEATH WORE A SMART LITTLE OUTFIT

A Berkley Prime Crime Book / published by arrangement with the author

PRINTING HISTORY
Berkley Prime Crime edition / June 1997

All rights reserved.
Copyright © 1997 by Orland Outland.
This book may not be reproduced in whole or in part, by mimeograph or any other means, without permission.
For information address: The Berkley Publishing Group, 200 Madison Avenue, New York, NY 10016.

The Putnam Berkley World Wide Web site address is
http://www.berkley.com

ISBN: 0-425-15855-1

Berkley Prime Crime Books are published
by The Berkley Publishing Group,
200 Madison Avenue, New York, NY 10016.
The name BERKLEY PRIME CRIME and the BERKLEY PRIME CRIME
design are trademarks belonging to Berkley Publishing Corporation.

PRINTED IN THE UNITED STATES OF AMERICA

10 9 8 7 6 5 4 3 2 1

ONE

As IT WAS SUPPOSED TO, BINKY'S ALARM WENT OFF AT 6 A.M.; as she was not supposed to, she turned it off and went back to sleep. She woke up several hours later, and, as usual, she debated whether or not to call in sick. Then she remembered that she was out of sick time, out of vacation time, and her boss was out of patience with her. Not to mention that her trust fund check for this quarter, which would have eased the financial pain of an unpaid day off on her next paycheck, had still failed to arrive. So she did get up, albeit grudgingly, and decided that since she was going to be late now anyway, she might as well be really late and enjoy the morning, as late was late, no matter how late, right? She searched desultorily for a robe and couldn't find one, so she went down to the lobby of her building in the buff.

Her paper wasn't there. "Naturally," she muttered.

Her feet were freezing on the marble floor of the lobby. "I've caught pneumonia for nothing." The clatter of dress shoes coming down the steps two at a time told her that her neighbor Jacob was leaving for work, which meant her clock was slow and she was even later than she thought.

At the top of the stairs, Jacob saw her and stopped. "You're going to catch your death of cold, running around in bare feet."

"My goddamn paper didn't come!" she screamed.

Jacob smoothed his suit and clattered down the stairs, his Cole Haans drowning out whatever sage advice he might have been giving her.

"What?" she shouted over the din of his shoes.

He stopped at the bottom of the stairs. "I said, are you sure you paid for it this month? You forgot last month, remember?"

"Of course I did. I had the check in an envelope right by the door . . . underneath my keys," she ended with a moan, realizing what was in the envelope she had looked at with such perturbation the night before, sensing that it had some vaguely important purpose.

Jacob clucked and opened his briefcase. "Here, dear, take mine. And mail the check this morning, won't you?"

She kissed him on the cheek. "You're an angel."

He went on his way, calling back over his shoulder. "And you're a mess. Now don't forget again!" And the door clicked shut behind him.

2

Binky trudged up the stairs, cursing whoever had decided a quaint Victorian house chopped into apartments couldn't have a nice unquaint practical convenience like an elevator. Reaching her third-floor apartment, she turned on the electric stove, sat on the counter opposite, and waved her feet over the burner while pouring herself a cup of coffee. Miss Porter's had not done what it had promised to do, which had been to prepare her for a glittering social marriage, but walking around with books on your head gave you a sense of balance that proved handy in apartments warmed only by stove heat.

She took her coffee to the kitchen table, pulled up the blinds, and took in the city around her. She smiled, knowing as a native would that it was going to be a perfect day. The fog would last till ten, then the sun would come out and it would be bright and clear until around four.

She damned the working life and opened the paper, read Art Mill's column, "Dear Abby," Liz Smith, and the comics, and that done, she had read all she ever read of the *San Francisco Times*.

She showered, threw on a dress, combed her hair, and put on lipstick. She was as ready for work as she ever would be.

Which must have been why the phone rang at that very instant. Although all over town there were surely many young women Binky's age who, eager to get to their power jobs, would have cursed and answered it abruptly, Binky herself was not one of them. Work was not a source of satisfaction for her, only of income. A ringing phone was an excuse to drop her purse, take off her shoes, and pour another cup of coffee. She prayed it was Doan, who would keep her on the horn for an obscenely long time, instead of a more perfunctory caller who would be less willing to help postpone her inevitable trudge to work. "Hello?"

"Oh, you're there!" It was Doan, of course.

"Where else would I be?"

"Well, *work* was the answer I had in mind. It's not important, I'll talk to you later, bye!"

"Wait a minute, Doan," she said darkly. "I know you better than that. You thought I was at work, so you called my machine, even though you have my work number. That means you were going to tell me something you didn't want to tell me personally. Now spit it out."

He sighed. "I was calling to tell you that I wouldn't be coming by to clean today. See, I've got to . . ."

She cut him off. "Doan. I don't care. I've got that big party to go to, and I couldn't possibly drag a strange man home to a dirty apartment."

"Most people would object to the strange man part more than the dirty apartment part, don't you think, dearie?"

"Just get over here and do it," she growled. "I'm not saying I won't be your best friend anymore, but I am saying I won't pay you to be my part-time maid anymore. What on earth could *you* possibly have to do that could be more important?"

"Fired? Moi? God forbid. I'm sure I'd be thrown onto the dole without your generosity. All right, all right, I'll just cancel my little date with one of San Francisco's premiere socialites to clean your little love nest so you won't offend some strange man whom you'll never see again anyway."

"What socialite?" she asked. "No offense, m'dear, but I can't imagine any of those old birds having much to do with a drag queen."

"I am *not* a drag queen," Doan fumed. "I do *not* wear makeup, I do *not* pretend to be a woman. The fact that I wear women's clothing has much more to do with comfort and style than it does with sex. In case you never noticed, it's only very recently that men's clothes have been anything but hideous, so many years ago . . ."

"So many years ago you began wearing women's clothes, etc., etc. We've had this conversation before. Who is so important that you have to leave me in filth?"

She could hear him smiling. "Even you would never believe me."

It was true: Binky never would have believed him. Doan had known her since she'd moved to San Francisco six months before. As he enjoyed the rare luxury of riding in a chauffeur-driven limousine, he warmly recalled their meeting—the two of them reaching at the same time for the last bottle of Veuve Clicquot at the liquor store, and Doan smiling (while not letting go of the bottle) and saying, "I'm sorry, I believe that this is mine."

Binky (not letting go either) smiled back. "No, so sorry. Mine," she said with fierce possessiveness.

"I'd let you have it, except that I have a date tonight, and . . ."

"So do I," she countered.

"I'm sure you do," he said, his voice firming, "but my date is a man who will drink only the best . . ."

"Mine is a chef . . ."

". . . and is absolutely no good in the sack unless he's tipsy . . ."

". . . who can't get excited unless I rub strawberries soaked in this shit all over his naked torso . . ."

". . . but if he is, he can have five orgasms in a night . . ."

She shoved the bottle at him. "You win."

It wasn't that she didn't think him the believable sort, just that, as he cheerfully confessed, so far as she knew, Doan McCandler was an amusing person with no visible means of support; not a kept boy, just someone who always managed to live on other people's good graces in perpetua.

And while Doan was not a drag queen, she had, at first, been fairly certain that he was a woman. Doan wore his blondish hair long, his face and body were fairly hairless, and he wore loose dresses that didn't give away his hips' secrets. He had feline features; he wore no makeup, but had naturally bright cheeks and lips. When he'd had to practically hit her over the head with the truth, she hadn't believed him at first. Nor would she have believed now that he was getting in a limo to see someone who, although richer than God, was not one of those many people whose generosity provided his means of existence.

Had he told her that he couldn't clean her apartment because he was going to see Eleanor Van Owens Ambermere, old and dear friend . . . well, she would have made some smart comment and he would have been proud of her. Socialites at the level of La Ambermere did tend to associate with their own kind to the exclusion of almost everybody else in the universe save those who were financially dependent on their good graces. People like Doan were of no use to the rich, nor were the rich of enough use to Doan for him to feel it necessary to suck up to them. His relationship with Eleanor was strictly a friendship, a friendship he thought it best to keep to himself, at least for the time being.

Many people in San Francisco lived in stately homes. Some even lived in mansions. The Ambermeres lived in what could only be described as a pile at the very height of Pacific Heights. Rich people always live in the heights, when they can help it; a speed bump on California Street was transformed into Laurel Heights for the benefit of its wealthy occupants. It's a miracle any rich people live in New York,

Doan thought—so flat! How ever does one look down on the rest of humanity as they do here?

As for the house itself, suffice it to say it might have been better suited to Hollywood than San Francisco: Tudor whatnot in all directions, a turret here and a balcony there, peaked roofs capping a few of the towers, battlements topping others. Doan surmised there was probably about two square inches of backyard—but that was only a guess; he'd never gotten that far toward the back of the house without getting lost.

Charles Ambermere's trademark silver and black Rolls (license WHELRDELR) was not in the drive. Doan didn't think it would be. Eleanor's husband was not kindly disposed toward men in dresses and had made everyone well aware of that fact on many occasions. So Doan made it a strict policy to visit the Ambermere pile only when it was certain the master would be gone.

Frannie opened the door for him. "Late," was all she said as she walked away. Eleanor Ambermere's "nurse" was not a woman of many words. Those who attempted to draw her out soon came to be grateful for this. She had been Eleanor's companion, secretary, and social surrogate for decades now.

Today Doan ignored her criticism of his lack of punctuality and followed her up the stairs. Although she had, to an outsider's eye, the temperament of a shrew and the face of Nurse Ratchet, he knew her one soft spot in the world was for the seventy-two-year-old lady upstairs.

"Frannie?" the raspy voice asked from the open door at the end of the third-floor landing. "Who was at the door?"

"Queen of Sheba."

"Tell him he's late."

"Did."

Doan entered her boudoir and went to the side of the huge bed—what comes after king-size? he thought—and kissed the frail old lady on the cheek.

"Well, don't you look old and sick today."

She laughed, a sound somewhere between Lauren Bacall and incurable laryngitis.

"You have no idea how good I feel," she crowed.

"Yes, I do. Divorce does wonders for the glands."

She lit a cigarette. "Oh, you heard?"

"At the same time half a million people read it in the morning paper today," he said accusingly.

"Oh, that's right. I forgot to tell you it was coming so soon. So," she said, fluffing several pillows and propping herself up, "what do you think?" Doan wasn't really angry, she knew, just put out about not being the first one to hear.

He patted her arm. "Whatever makes you happy, dear."

"It makes me happy, believe me. When I think of all the years . . ." her eyes misted over, and she reached out for Doan's hand, which he quickly gave her.

9

All the years, Doan echoed to himself. He looked at the picture on the nightstand of the frail, beautiful young heiress, who had finally gotten married at the age of thirty-seven, already an old maid in most eyes. Charles Ambermere was poor, sexy, ambitious, twenty-one, and despised by her family. He went on to do marginally adequate things, all with her money, none of which ever generated a return. She had been grateful for his attentions, though they waned as she became wheelchair-bound in her forties and disappeared entirely when she became bedridden in her fifties. She'd become senile at sixty, and the unloving old gold digger had managed to have her ruled incompetent two years previously, and had been able to assume complete control of a sum so huge that even he could not squander it all.

Doan's introduction to her had come five years before, shortly after she had become what is known in nursing circles as "difficult," meaning that she liked to call a cab, sneak out of the house, and ride to the top of Russian Hill, from which she would coast down the hill in her wheelchair toward the wharf, in scenes that far surpassed those in *Bullitt*. One such day, Doan had been engaged in watching a fisherman in tight, faded jeans as he bent, lifted boxes, stepped high over the edge of his trawler, and set them down on the dock, when the screams of the crowd and a hoarse shout of glee finally diverted his attention. Eleanor was barreling toward him at God knew how many miles per hour.

Doan had never been what anyone might call butch, but he knew what to do in a crisis. He gauged her trajectory, got a running start beside the chair, grabbed the handles as she passed him, and ran with it to slow rather than stop it, as trying to stop it would have resulted in dislocated shoulders for him and a projectile passenger. Only inches from the water, tight, faded jeans grabbed the arms of the much-slowed chair and brought it to a complete halt, thus bringing to Doan Eleanor's friendship, mild notoriety, and a three-month liaison with tight, faded jeans, ended only by his strange and unfathomable (to Doan) desire to rejoin the Merchant Marines and see what parts of the world he hadn't already seen.

Eleanor was, in her dottiness, the perfect companion for Doan. Her madness had a method, there was no doubt of that. Her senility was a second childhood for a woman who'd never really had a first one. She would come up with the most outrageous whims— one day, the third day of nonstop rain, she had decided that she wanted to see Tahiti—immediately. And she'd had the means to fulfill these whims (not wanting to transfer planes in Hawaii, she'd ordered her solicitors to purchase an airplane—immediately—and have it ready for her—immediately). She asked nothing of Doan, and he nothing of her, other than mutual companionship and amusement. He went along with her on everything because being in on her massive-scale frivolities was, he surmised, as close to heaven as he'd ever get.

When Charles wrested away control over her money, it was the end of all those festivities. She became cranky, hypochondriac, shrill, whiny—in short, old. Doan felt it was his duty to make her retain some links with the world she had not begun to enjoy until so late in life, the world she had been able to view the way a child does—the whole thing one big toy for her to play with. Even in her darkest days, he would come to see her and make her laugh. It was not out of charity; Doan did not possess the do-gooding soul of a candy striper. He had come to love Eleanor, and while he believed the doctors when they said she'd never be her fun-loving self again, he stuck with her through the dark times as she'd stuck with him through her good times.

And then, several months ago, it had started to happen.

Frannie, no spring chicken herself, almost had a coronary at the sight: Eleanor Van Owens Ambermere, walking, yes, walking into the kitchen and making a peanut butter and jelly sandwich. "Well?" she had asked in the husky voice that had always seemed so out of place in the senile little old lady. "You got a problem with this?" she had demanded as she waved the sandwich around the room.

Such lucid moments became more and more frequent, as did her trips out of bed. Charles Ambermere, finally concerned about his wife's health, ordered up a fleet of doctors. Three of them had concluded that, as doctors will, they could make no conclusions without further tests. That was when Eleanor had raised her voice to the decibel level suitable to Biblical jeremiads and ordered them out of the house.

And now that Eleanor was awake and alert nearly all of the time, healthy as an ox for the first time in her life (in bed today only due to a slight cold), and had just been certified sane and competent to manage her own affairs by five psychiatrists, she had filed for divorce. And she had every intention of making sure Charles Ambermere didn't get a cent beyond the kajillions he'd already blown.

"Well," Doan said, "those days are all over now. And all things considered, they weren't all bad."

"Yeah," she agreed, lighting another cigarette. She was regenerating so completely and quickly, she was afraid of losing her raspy voice (which she felt gave her character), so she had started smoking, arguing forcefully that now that she was so indecently healthy, she had a right to at least one vice. "I remember how I met you. It was in Paris during the war. You were with the Resistance . . . or were you a Nazi . . . ?" She leaned back in the bed and frowned, trying to remember.

Doan smiled and waited patiently, knowing this was one of her more and more infrequent trips and that it would be over quickly.

She sat up, blinking furiously. "No. It was at the wharf. People ran to get out of my way, you ran after me in those Manolo Blahnik shoes you never *would* loan me, and I ran smack into that gorgeous fisher-

13

man. No wonder I went back to la-la land for a minute; the truth is so goddamn surreal, the Nazi story was more likely." She was, Doan noted approvingly, no longer infuriated by her lapses, knowing as he did that they would soon be completely a thing of the past. "Whatever happened to him?"

"He threw me over for a life of cheap thrills in far-flung ports. I think he's a writer now."

"Oh? What does he write?"

"All about cheap thrills in far-flung ports, I daresay. For magazines we would not want in our homes. Anyway, you wanted to see me, my dear?"

"Yes. Pour me a drink, will you." Doan obeyed, ignoring Frannie's frown. If you are seventy-two, he believed, there is no reason to worry about moderation, as chances are you will drop dead any second anyway. "I need your help."

"And you always have it."

"There's money in it for you."

"I adore money, and did you know that you're the one person I know who I've never gotten any out of?"

"I want you to take . . ." she pulled back her comforter to reveal four bulky manila envelopes, ". . . these to the locations specified on them, deposit them there, and not ask any questions."

Doan hiked several miles to the other side of the bed and picked one up. "Good lord, did you type *War and Peace* over for fun? Eleanor, these addresses . . . Geneva, Bermuda, Paris, London?"

She handed him his tickets. "Here ya go, kiddo. All-expenses-paid trip to fun capitals of the world, courtesy of Eleanor Van Owens . . . Ambermere," she added the last word as an unpleasant after-thought.

"What's in them?"

"No questions."

"Oh, crap, come off it! This is Doan! You are asking me, the world's biggest gossip, to do something without knowing what it's all about?"

"You're putting four copies of the same set of papers in safe places around the world. Can you leave tomorrow? And I made Bermuda the last stop, figured that was where you'd probably want to loiter awhile, but the rest of them have got to get deposited fairly quickly."

Doan sighed. "You want me to just drop everything and . . . go."

"Yeah. If you would, please."

"Ah! You said please! About time!"

She narrowed her eyes to regard him. "Yes, Doan. Please do this for me. Please spend time in the great capitals of the world. Please spend the ten thousand dollars you'll find in that envelope behind the tickets."

Doan choked. "What! Now, I really don't need that kind of money. I don't want it. After all, how fast can you spend it, really? Real fast, sure, if you start. But I'd look at it, and then I'd think, I really should invest this. And do you know what would happen

15

then? I'd have to go visit my broker to see how my money was doing, and I couldn't wear a dress, because you can dress like this if you're very rich, and no one will mess with you because you're rich, and you can dress like this if you're very poor, because people expect colorful characters, as they would describe me, to be poor—but if you were suddenly middle-class and dressed like this, why, they'd lock you up!"

She smiled. "Cheer up. There are casinos in Bermuda, so you can lose some of it, and some of the most gorgeous men go there to find someone to take care of them for a while, so you can spend some on them."

"Me, supporting someone else? What a novel idea!"

"Then you'll do it."

He realized he had been caught completely off guard. "Only if I know what I'm carrying. Are you a Communist plant, who's spent all these years faking illness as part of your deep cover? Am I taking secrets out of the country?"

"Let's just say that they have something to do with my divorce. And that I may not need them. They're a record of all of Charles's little indiscretions. I started it when I was semisane, before he knew I was getting better. I spied on him in his study, recorded his phone calls, all sorts of good stuff. So, if anything happens to me, there's the evidence to put him away. And in case anything happens to you between here and

Europe, God forbid of course, I've got the originals in a safe place here that only I know about."

"Eleanor! Do you really think he'd kill you?"

Her face became grave. "If you knew Charles like I know Charles, you wouldn't ask."

"So why have you waited to put these papers in safe places?"

"Because he agreed to my terms of divorce last week."

"What? Then why do I have to . . ."

"Because it was too easy. That means Charles has got money from somewhere else. From some shady operation he's got going. You see, I lied to him. I told him the papers were already hidden away. I also didn't tell him about everything I've got on him. Now it seems to be advisable to actually do it."

"Why don't we just kill him?" Doan said, having extremely catholic tastes in justice and not being wild about the idea that he might meet with a bad end on this errand. Frannie grunted her approval of this idea.

"Because," she explained, "I want him to suffer."

Doan smiled. "Now, that's my kind of reasoning: revenge as an art form."

Frannie's sixth sense stirred her. "Ambermere's back."

"Uh-oh," Doan said. "Is there a back exit?"

"Sure, to the backyard. This is San Francisco, Doan, nobody has a back exit that doesn't lead into somebody else's house."

"Somebody else's house wouldn't be so bad, if Charles weren't in it."

"I'll protect you," Frannie swore, and they made their way out.

"Call me from your stops," Eleanor shouted after him. "I want to be sure you haven't gotten distracted by that cash—or some man."

"No distractions until business is taken care of," Doan promised.

And even though Charles Ambermere came through the door while Doan and Frannie were still on the Scarlett O'Hara staircase, the thought of $10,000 with no bills attached had left Doan feeling warm as toast. "Hello, there," he said jauntily.

Ambermere looked up, surprise quickly replaced by a scowl. "Oh, it's you."

"C'est moi!" Doan corrected him, thinking of his imminent trip to Europe. "Sorry to hear about the divorce," he added, unable to help himself.

Although handsome in youth, Charles Ambermere was not now a good-looking man even in the best lighting and on his good behavior, and hadn't been for some twenty alcoholic years. His bespoke suits concealed his paunch and narrow shoulders, his glossy silver hair was expensively maintained at prices that would have made a Trump blush, and yet, nothing could be done short of major plastic surgery for that face; a sour, red-nosed complexion, blobby lips pursed in disapproval . . . think of Santa Claus laid off and forced into a one-room apartment in the bad part of town, drinking away his Social Security check, and that's what Charles's face looked like.

He pointed at Doan. "You . . . one day . . . will get what's coming to you."

Doan brightened. "I do hope so! Well, it's been nice seeing you. Good-bye!" he added, enjoying the pleasure of looking down on the five-foot-six Charles as he passed him by.

"What are you looking at," Charles demanded of Frannie, who was smirking on the stairs.

"Guess," she said, leaving him to his humiliation and rage.

Binky worked as a clerical cog at the San Francisco Police Department, a job that completely mortified her well-to-do Main Line relatives, who were, however, not mortified enough to liberate her trust fund and enable her to live without a job. The purpose of her grandfather's will had been to see to it that all his granddaughters had good allowances to supplement their husband's incomes—for they would all, of course, have wealthy husbands of good family. Binky had not married, the family disapproved of this state of affairs, and so the trust money continued as a trickle rather than a flood. This unpleasant state of affairs resulted in Binky's requiring permanent employment—something her early life had not prepared her for, since having to toil at some drudgy job was not what her kind were ever supposed to even think of having to do. Had she not been forced by childhood teachers to learn how to type (her hand-writing being unladylike in the extreme), she would now not have even had this minimal skill to use in defying the dictates of the Van de Kamps.

She growled in response to her fellow employees' hellos, poured a cup of coffee, and sat down at her desk. A sip of coffee reassured her that her chances of living through the morning were good. Then Julie showed up. "Hi!"

If they still made them, Binky thought, Julie would be a perfect Mouseketeer. Dealing with perky people with no problems was not one of Binky's strong points.

"Hello, Julie," she sighed.

"Hey, did you see this morning's *Times*?" Julie asked her.

"Belatedly, yeah."

"Did you read about what that crazy Mrs. Am-bermere's done now?" she asked breathlessly.

"If it wasn't in Art's column or Liz's, then no, I didn't."

Julie sighed theatrically, cheered by the opportunity to berate someone sillier than herself. "Honestly, Binky, I don't understand you. You're a Woman of the Nineties," Julie pronounced with the reverence Binky felt should be used only for words like *Gaultier* or *heavy cream*. "You should be informed about the world around you."

"Julie, I can tell you any day's news in one sentence:

a plane has crashed, people are poorer, taxes are higher, someone's at war."

"Saw it," Lisa said. "Sued for divorce." Lisa had been there longer than any of them, and the absence of proper articles in the police reports she typed all day had affected her powers of speech.

"What!" Binky asked, shocked.

"Good," Mark, the only male typist, said with great satisfaction. "Old man Ambermere will be broke after he pays the alimony she'll get out of him, the way he's treated her. It was all her money to start with, you know."

Julie got indignant. "You don't think that poor man has suffered at her hands? What with her crazy stunts and the way she went through all that money on her trips and the way she was always being brought home by the police? Think of what she could have done for the poor, homeless people with all that money. . . ." Binky allowed the low drone to find its proper place in the back of her mind as she began the day's work.

Mark lit a cigarette, saw the hungry look on Binky's face, and tossed her one. "What are you doing this weekend?" He was always eager to silence Julie, had been ever since he'd casually mentioned his boyfriend on his first day of work two weeks ago, and Julie had not nearly as casually informed him that accepting Jesus into his heart could save him from the depraved life that was leading him straight to hell.

"I was saying," Julie continued, "that . . ."

"I'm going to sleep till noon, then have some pastry delivered, then chill a bottle of champagne, read a Wodehouse novel while eating and drinking my goodies, listen to some extremely loud classical music, and then go out to dinner with some gorgeous man, whom I have not yet met."

"Ohhh . . ." Mark moaned, more at the thought of the day alone with all of life's luxuries than at the thought of the man. As was the case with so many people in the city these days, food had effectively replaced sex as the primary deliverer of earthly delight. "Yes, oh, yes! Do it to me now!" he shouted, mentally adding a fresh, hot loaf of sourdough bread split down the middle with a stick of butter shoved inside it. As was also the case with most people, food had so effectively replaced sex (that, really, had been so boring most of the time, whereas pastry from the right bakery never failed to deliver the big O) that one was prone to use the terminology of one in reference to the other.

"There's no smoking in public buildings as of January first," Julie reminded them.

"Well then," Binky said, "I'll just have to chain-smoke between now and then to get ahead of the game."

Julie made a sound of disgust and went to work.

Later that morning, Mark got a call. "Oh, God," he moaned. "I've got to go see Old Rotgut." Sympathy was dispensed by all but Julie.

Sergeant Seamus Flaharity's alcoholic incompetence endeared him to many of his fellow officers, for reasons we shall not attempt to fathom. A sergeant for twenty of his thirty years on the force, politics dictated he would go no farther—to the chief of police, he was a priceless asset in the conservative parts of town, but elsewhere in the city he was a embarrassment. His well-known fondness for cheap whiskey, coupled with his enormous stomach (the rest of him being quite skinny, in silhouette he looked like a yam mounted on toothpicks), had earned him his nickname.

Binky was caught up on her fellow employees' lives and the best office gossip by ten, and, not seeing any point in doing any work, was ready to go home. This not being fiscally possible, she decided to amble by Rotgut's office and see if she could pick up a thread of the conversation.

She took her cup with her and stood at the water cooler outside his door. She heard Mark's indignant voice first.

". . . can't fire me!"

". . . whatever I want."

". . . sue you . . . discrimination . . ."

". . . little fag, listen up . . ."

"Little fag! You asshole, you . . ."

". . . not the one . . . up the ass . . ."

Binky turned tail and ran. Too ugly for words.

Mark stormed back in and slammed the door, which caused Julie to spill her herb tea.

"I've just been fired!"

"I know. I overheard every other word of it."

"I can't believe this. This is San Francisco, for God's sake. People don't get fired for eating dogs or smoking dope or screwing sheep."

"They do if they work for the Police Department," Julie crowed, tossing her head. "We have an image to maintain."

Mark looked at her with disbelief, then shook his head. He grabbed his coat and flew out the door.

Julie sighed. "Don't worry about him, Binky. They're used to getting fired. I have to say I'm glad, though."

"Why? What the hell did he ever do to you?"

"Well, you know. I mean . . . well, I've been worried lately. About AIDS. And being around a . . . homosexual," she accomplished the death-defying feat of compressing the word into one syllable, as if saying it too slowly could make her one. "He's probably got it. They've probably all got it."

Binky smiled. "Julie?"

"Yes?" she answered brightly.

"It's amazing that though I've worked with you for six months, until now I never realized what a truly ignorant bitch you are."

Julie's eyes widened, her lower lip trembled, and then she burst into tears. Lisa rolled her eyes and went back to work.

Binky got up and walked behind Julie. "I'm sorry." She kissed Julie on the top of her head, then she whispered in her ear. "I kissed a homosexual this morning, Julie. So I'm sure he gave me AIDS. I sure hope I didn't just give it to *you*."

She crossed her arms and watched with satisfaction as Julie ran screaming down the hall, tearing out huge clumps of her hair and begging for someone to bleach her body.

Binky caught up with Mark in the parking lot, where he was smoking furiously.

"Looks like fun," she said.

"What?"

"Smoking furiously. Let me have a ciggie." He handed her one, which she lit off the end of his.

"Be careful," he spat bitterly. "I might give you AIDS."

"Oh, did you hear that?"

"Every other word."

"Don't worry. I assure you, I gave Julie her just desserts. So what are you going to do now?"

"Right now I'm going to wait for Roy to come pick me up."

"Call him back. Tell him not to bother. We'll do lunch."

"It's ten o'clock!"

"Brunch, then."

"Can you afford to treat? 'Cause the unemployed can't afford such things."

"Don't worry. Such crises are what charge cards are for." She sighed. "Besides, you can get another job. Or you can sue and they'll give you this one back

rather than fork out a huge discrimination settlement. You want to hear crisis? Real crisis? My two
best friends are coming over later today."

"So where's the crisis?"

"Oh, it's just that neither knows the other will be
there and they . . . well, sort of hate each other's
guts."

Doan came through Binky's door at three that afternoon, humming a Rodgers and Hart tune. He screamed
at the sight of Binky flopped on the couch with a
cigarette in one hand and a pulpy novel in the other.
"What are you doing here?!"

Binky turned to see him in his French maid's
uniform, replete with white cap, short black dress
with white frilled front, and sensible shoes.

As he stomped indignantly toward her, she felt a
stab of jealousy that he looked even better in skirts
than she did. The uniform almost made her laugh.
No one was less dainty or subservient than Doan. His
light brown bangs flopped over his brow as he
stormed toward her, his ice-gray eyes burning holes in
her lazy body.

"You are supposed to be at work. That's our
arrangement. I come in to clean when you're not here
to get in my way. Out!"

Binky didn't move. "Cute outfit."

"Puts me in the spirit of things." He towered over
her, six feet two inches of pissed-off part-time ser-
vant. "Out!"

"Skip the couch today, okay?"

"Skip it? No way. I'm a perfectionist. Besides, the spare change I get from under the cushions is almost as much as my pitiful pay."

"What do you expect to get for one day a week?"

"Eighteen thousand dollars a year. Enough for my own American Express card. It's tedious using other people's; you never know when they're going to get sick of you and cancel it. I remember once I was getting some Clinique at Macy's, and they called it in and . . ."

As he spoke, Doan sat down across from her, crossed his legs, and opened one of her sodas. She cut him off. "Are you working today or not?"

He lowered his head, arched his eyebrows to give himself room to look at her, and puckered his mouth. The whole effect said, "My, aren't we testy today?"

"Because if you are, you'd better start. KC's coming over."

Doan shrieked and flew out of the chair. "How could you?" He began wielding the feather duster like a machete around the apartment, stopping at the table to dust the fallen ashes from Binky's cigarette onto the floor. Convinced Binky wasn't watching, he furtively scuffed them into the carpet.

The doorbell rang. "AAAAAAKKK! It's here!"

Binky didn't move. "You're the maid; answer the door."

Doan opened the door and curtsied to the waiting

27

KC. "Alors, m'sieur. Comment allez-vous? Como esta usted? May I take your dead cow, señor?"

KC shook his head and walked past Doan. "Hey, Binky." He smiled, shaking his head, his dark brown eyes twinkling with amusement as they always did at the sight of Doan.

"Did you . . . you look different," she said.

He rubbed his crewcut head. "Got a haircut."

"Which hair did you cut?" Doan asked, whipping past KC and giving his crewcut head a few quick brushes with the duster.

Binky sighed. It was no use telling them not to get on each other's nerves. The only thing the two of them had in common was an inordinate love of gossip. She plunged ahead.

"Remember Mark?" she asked. Doan put a hand to his forehead and sighed. "That gorgeous man you work with." His tone darkened abruptly. "The one you told me was married. I gave up on him and then I find out that he's married to another man!"

"So what's the difference?" she asked him.

"The difference is that straight men are off limits. All gay men are fair game. Especially when they move into an apartment within walking distance of the Castro."

"Anyway," she cut him off, "he got fired today by Old Rotgut."

Another thing the two of them had in common was a severe hatred of Sergeant Flaharity. "That jerk. I bet it was because he's gay," KC decided.

"You got it."

Doan shook his head. "Why do they let that creature out of its cage?" Both of them had been harassed by Flaharity and his friends more than once. While there was one faction in the SFPD that tried to keep good relations with the gay community, most cops were still pretty bigoted. You always knew when something had brought Flaharity or one of his cronies into the Castro, because enrollment in self-defense courses rocketed the next day. San Francisco's police department was still predominantly composed of white Irish cops whose fathers had been cops, and whose grandfathers had been cops, etc., etc. And it did not help that many of these Irish cops were also members of the Holy Roman Catholic Church, an institution that, while it no longer feels secure publicly endorsing the burning of homosexuals at the stake, nonetheless maintains an artful silence in the face of violence against sinners.

"So what's he gonna do?" KC asked.

"Poor thing," Doan empathized. "He can stay with me."

"He has a home," Binky reminded him.

"Maybe not for long," Doan hoped fervently. "Maybe hubby will kick him out when the rent comes due and . . ."

"God, you're such a cynic," KC shot.

"No, I'm an optimist. I wait for terrible things to happen to other people, and then everything they have falls into my lap."

"Good things come to those who wait," Binky reproved.

"Yeah, yeah. But a good shove in the right direction doesn't hurt."

"Why don't we organize a protest?" KC suggested.

Doan gave him a distrustful eye. "Are you suggesting we carry signs and shout and otherwise look frightfully undecorative in front of television cameras, so that all our friends and relatives can see us having a tantrum? All of which must be prefaced by about six hundred meetings presided over by angry young men who look like affronted insects in their little round glasses? Are you suggesting that I listen for hours to someone (who ought to be packed off from the Finland Station sealed up in the great train of historical necessity) as he talks about hammering out our politics? Besides, any time some group like that becomes effective, it just gets taken over by a bunch of Commies with their own agenda."

KC looked at him sideways. "I can't believe you've ever heard of the great train of historical necessity."

Doan sighed and crossed his legs. "You think any intellectual bent I might have is invalidated by the fact that I like to wear a dress."

"The first time I saw you, you were doing Gloria Swanson in a drag show. That is not a healthy testament to your mental skills."

"I've never seen you dressed like Gloria Swanson," Binky said, mad at missing out again.

"You never saw the stupid drag show I did," Doan informed her.

"If it was a stupid drag show, why did you do it?" KC asked.

"Taste, charm, and wit do not pay the rent. It is merely something I got good at back when I was a screaming queen and enjoyed such things. It also beats working a counter at Macy's."

"Well, no offense, but you are, after all . . . a drag queen."

He turned to Binky. "Didn't we just have this conversation?"

"What were we talking about?" Binky asked, trying to remember what it was she had been about to say.

KC thought about it for a minute. "Let's see . . . we started with your friend getting fired, then about Rotgut, then Doan on love and sex, then Doan on politics, then Doan on paying the rent . . ."

Doan leaned back with a satisfied sigh. "Just the kind of trivial, pointless conversation I adore!"

Binky jumped up. "Oh! You'll be delighted to know that I heard something that actually appeared in the news today!"

"No!" Doan and KC chorused.

"Yes. I heard Eleanor Ambermere's getting divorced!"

They leaned back into their seats. "That," KC informed her, "is not exactly what I'd call hard news."

"True," Doan agreed, bursting to tell them the whole story but sworn to secrecy by Eleanor. "Far more important than hard news, but hard to miss hearing."

"Well," she said indignantly, "I also heard the cops have a lead on the SoMa Killer."

Doan shrugged. "So? Who cares about someone who goes around murdering artists? I thought artists were supposed to be poor! So why is it every time they move into a neighborhood, all of a sudden no one else can afford to live there? So who in their right mind wants him caught? You know how in mysteries there's always one character who says, 'I didn't do it, but if I met the guy who did, I'd thank him'? God, in this city there will be ten thousand people saying that. They could make a whole season's worth of *Murder, She Wrote*. Watch Angela Lansbury questioning all those hysterical welfare mothers who've lost their apartments and see how fast her patience runs out. That show is pretty silly, anyway. I mean, she lays out the method of murder to the killer, and he confesses and gets arrested, even when she does it when there's no one else around. No one ever beats her up and makes a run for it. That's TV for you. In real life, her ass would be dead meat by now!"

"Doan," Binky interrupted. "You're digressing."

"You know another thing about that show?" he continued obliviously. "Here's this mystery writer, for God's sake, and everyone's heard of her! Even that guy in the KGB had read all her books. Come on! The

32

only famous mystery writers anymore are the ones who do those stupid spy thrillers. I mean, if she was Agatha Christie, okay, everyone's heard of Agatha Christie. But you know it's not, because she jogs, and can you see Agatha Christie jogging?"

Binky sighed. "Doan, I realize now why I keep you around."

"Really? Do tell."

"Every time I feel like I'm out of touch with reality, I can always turn and see you and know there's someone even further out of touch than I am."

"That's a lovely thought, dear." He got up and began idly dusting again.

"What am I going to wear to that party tomorrow night?" she asked.

"Do you want to borrow something of mine?" Doan asked.

"Hmmm . . . yeah, I'll take a look at what you've got."

"Of course," Doan added, "if you really wanted to cause a splash, you should borrow something of his," he concluded, pointing dramatically at KC.

"Is this your cop party?" KC asked her.

"It's the Annual Police Department Charity Ball," she corrected him. "And I go because I can meet a cute policeman from another station and take him home and sleep with him, secure in the knowledge that it won't get around that I'm a slut."

"Are you?" Doan asked.

"Never you mind."

"How do you know it won't get around?" KC asked.

"Simple. I lie. I tell him I'm some muckety-muck's secretary. Then if he goes and brags about how he slept with so-and-so's secretary, well . . . I always pick someone mean and ugly to impersonate."

Doan screamed. "And then someone who knows who she is laughs at him, tells him how mean and ugly she is, and no matter how hard he denies it, they'll believe it was her! You're so cruel!"

KC frowned. "Hell of a trick to play on a guy you sleep with."

"Hey," she shrugged, "if he keeps his mouth shut, no big deal. If he brags about his conquests, then he deserves all the shit they can pile on him."

"Haven't you ever been really mean to a man?" Doan asked KC.

He thought about it. "Well, once. Kind of. This really unpleasant man . . ."

"You mean 'this horrid old troll,'" Doan corrected him.

KC frowned. "I don't use that word. Anyway, this very unpleasant man came up to me in a bar, pointed at his friend and said, 'My friend over there bet me you wouldn't give me the time of day.' Well, I told him I was just leaving and gave him a phone number and told him to call it sometime."

"A number?" Binky asked. "What number?"

"Time, of course."

"I didn't think you had it in you," Doan said.

"Had what in me?"

"A mean streak."

KC only smiled.

Doan sighed. "I love calling time. I love the time lady. Whenever I get depressed, I just call the time lady. 'The time is . . . five forty-seven . . . exactly!' She's so thrilled that it's exactly five forty-seven. How can you be depressed when there are people out there who are happy just knowing what time it is?"

KC sighed. "You're trivial, Doan."

"Whimsical. The word is whimsical." He placed the feather duster on KC's head and came around to study the effect.

"I don't think it's me," KC opined.

"You're right. You need to shave the moustache."

KC tossed the duster at him. Doan shrieked and ducked. "Well! That's it, I'm leaving. I'll be back tomorrow. To clean." He glared at Binky. "While you're gone. Now I'm going to go home and put on a simple frock and go shopping. Bonjour, madame et señor." He grabbed his purse and was out the door.

KC shuddered. "I think I'm coming down with something."

"Oh, really? You seem fine to me."

"Yeah. But I think I actually enjoyed having him around."

"Oh, my God! We'll get you to bed and give you some aspirin and some orange juice."

He laughed. "I'm fine, really. I came over to talk to you about your finances, actually."

Binky sighed and fell back on the couch. "Must we?"

"If you're to have any finances, we must."

Binky had not regretted hiring KC to be her accountant; she'd wanted someone who'd watch over her profligacy and keep her from total bankruptcy, and she'd gotten that, and a good friend to boot. It was just . . . so depressing to talk about money, at least when she didn't have any.

KC pulled some papers out of his bag. "Now, about some of these bills . . ."

"Uh-oh. I think I know which ones you've got there."

"Three hundred seventy-two dollars and fifty cents at the Castro Day Spa? On Visa, no less?"

"I was . . . short of cash that day."

"Which explains why you also spent eighty-seven dollars and ninety-five cents at Le Marcel Hair Design? Excuse me, Binky, but . . . you've got a *bob*. Does a bob really require eighty-seven ninety-five worth of 'design'?"

"I suppose you'd only really be happy if I cut it myself," she said, lighting an imported cigarette.

"If Supercuts is good enough for the cast of *Friends*, it's good enough for you."

"Hmph," Binky replied, at a loss for a rejoinder to that.

"Look, Binky. You get thirty thousand a year from your trust. You shouldn't have to work some demeaning job you hate, if you'd just manage your finances a little better."

"Why don't you invest those finances of mine in some unknown software company and make me a millionairess, and then I wouldn't have to worry about running out of cash?"

"If you ever left enough cash in your account for me to invest, I would. Instead, you act like the ATM is just . . . a place to get more free money when you run out."

Her eyes widened. "It isn't?"

He sighed. "I give up. I see now why you're such good friends with Doan."

"Why's that?"

"You're just like him."

"I'll take that as a compliment." She proferred a dish. "Caviar?"

"Well, it's already bought and paid for, so I might as well." It had actually been charged on her Visa, and thus bought but not actually paid for, but she discreetly saw fit not to fill him in.

She smiled. "Enjoy, darling. It's the only good that ever came from the wealth of the Van de Kamps."

TWO

$\mathcal{B}$INKY HID IN A DOORWAY ALONGSIDE DAVIES SYMPHONY Hall, where the policemen's ball was already in full swing. She grabbed the front of Doan's black, strapless cocktail dress and pulled it out as far as she could, getting a few deep breaths before gently letting it pull itself back into place, knowing full well that if she just let go, the damn thing would snap back and cut off her breasts. She cursed Doan for forcing her into it. "Suck in that gut!" he'd commanded, "flex those tits! We'll make it fit!" Attempts to explain the difference between the male and female hip structures had fallen on deaf ears. As far as Doan was concerned, if they could wear each other's airy summer dresses, then they wore the same size in evening gowns. But what fit Doan gripped Binky like a boa constrictor. She didn't dare look down at the dress when she stepped out of the doorway and back onto the street—the flash of streetlights off the sequins would blind her.

She dug her ticket out of her purse and surrendered it at the door, checked her wrap, and walked directly to the bar in short, careful steps, terrified of ruining the dress. She was already sweating by the time she got to the bar. "I'm wearing a goddamn sauna suit," she muttered.

"Looks more like asbestos Saran Wrap to me," the bartender confided. She fell in love with the sound of his voice, but then she looked up and saw the crewcut and moustache. It may not be true, she sighed, that all the good ones are gay—just all the amusing ones.

She got her drink and left the bar in search of attractive and unfamiliar men. Her efforts seemed to be for naught until she caught sight of something tall and dark in a tuxedo. She threaded her way across the hall, avoiding people she knew who might corral her into conversation and cause her to lose sight of the glittering prize.

"Oh, my," she whispered from her vantage point behind a huge floral arrangement. Tall and Dark was at the bar talking to the mayor. He was about six foot four, black hair, sharp features, and an olive complexion. Furthermore, Binky's practiced eye told her from his hands and jawline alone that he had an incredible body.

A fat personage blocked what view she'd had. She cursed and got ready to dash just as soon as the mayor left Tall and Dark alone.

"I can't believe it!" a booming voice from behind her declared. She grabbed a compact out of her purse and pretended to check her makeup as the source of so much bluff heartiness passed her by to clap a hand on the shoulder of the fat obstacle. "If it isn't Sergeant Flaharity looking like a penguin!"

Flaharity! The last person she wanted to talk to! She ducked, unladylike, behind a huge flower arrangement that looked like it had already seen two funerals before this party.

"Well, now, Mr. Ambermere, you aren't exactly looking fit and trim yourself!"

"Ho! Ho! Ho!"

The dialogue continued in this fascinating vein for a while, and Binky was about to make for the bar again when Ambermere nudged Rotgut with his elbow, pointing his drink at Tall and Dark. "Get a load of that." Binky leaned into the flowers to hear better.

"Yeah, I see." Rotgut muttered.

"Goddamn fags are everywhere."

Oh, no! she thought. One candidate for my charms, and he's another sister. Damn it! I'm going home.

The two charmers bid each other their adieus, and Binky discovered that her head was quite entangled in the floral arrangement. As she struggled to get out, a hand reached in. "Can I help you with that?" the deep, silky voice asked.

"Only if you have a pair of pruning shears in your pocket."

"Here, hold still." Confident, capable hands brushed her neck and neatly unknotted the flowers. She laid her trauma aside to check the left hand for a wedding ring and found none, always a promising sign. She pulled her head out.

"Nice hands," she complimented him before turning around to face him. "Oh, damn!" It was T and D.

"Sorry to disappoint you," he smiled, and extended his hand. "Name's Luke."

"Binky," she replied.

"You sure don't look like a Binky."

"Thank you. If there's anything I'm not, it's preppy."

"If there's anything I'm not, it's biblical." He finally let go of her hand. "See you around."

"Bye," she crooned, the way she'd seen Kathleen Turner do it, or as close as she could with the breath the dress allowed her to take in. She sighed, watching him walk away. "That man," she said aloud, "is not gay." She felt something sticking to her palm and opened her hand to find a piece of paper with a neatly written phone number.

"Nice trick!" she murmured.

Being smart enough to realize that after that one, any other man would be far too pale in comparison, she pulled the dress out, fanned her breasts, eased it back into place, tucked the precious piece of paper into her purse, and went to fetch her wrap.

She entered her apartment to find Doan sprawled on her couch watching TV, wearing one of her silk negligees, which barely covered his privates.

"Home so soon?" he asked. "Didn't expect to see you until tomorrow, if then."

"What are you watching?" she asked, ignoring the comment.

Doan yawned and stretched, the negligee creeping up over his genitals. Binky threw her wrap over him just in time.

"Thank you, I needed a blanket. Have a good time with the straight boys? Give your number to Mr. Goodbar?"

"No. Got a number, though."

"Is that all?"

"You should have seen what gave it to me. Six four, dark hair, olive skin, and would you believe blue eyes?"

Doan leapt off the couch. "Give me that."

She clutched her purse to her bosom, slipping into Joan Crawford mode. "He's my man, and I'll fight to keep him."

"Okay, okay." He retreated to the kitchen.

"Since you decided to use your housekeeping key to come over and watch my cable TV, did you answer the phone and did you bother to take any messages?"

"Two calls. It, and the dreamboat."

"KC?"

"Yes. It. He's coming over tomorrow morning to

look at some figures. Why you trust that man with your money is beyond me."

"First, because the only thing I learned to balance in school was a book on my head. Second, he is an accountant. I take it the dreamboat was Mark? What did he say?"

"Oh, he just called to say hi."

"Come on, Doan. Mark wouldn't just call to say hi."

"Don't worry. He had a problem, but I took care of it." He smiled sweetly.

"Out with it."

Doan sailed past her. "Oh, he and his . . . husband? Yes. They had a little tiff and he needed somewhere to stay."

"You didn't."

"He was just here fifteen minutes ago. To pick up the keys to my apartment. After all, he didn't want to stay here without your permission, and Lord knows when you'd get home, and with what. Well, I've got to be going. I've got . . . something in the oven."

Binky laughed as she went into her bedroom and removed the dress, exaggerating her relief for Doan's benefit.

"Stop that," he commanded from the couch. "You looked wonderful, and you know it."

"Sure, and the price was damage to my lungs equivalent to two thousand packs of cigarettes. And if I ever have a child, I am now incapable of breast-feeding."

"Flat tits are in this year anyway; yours were too big."

"Only for you, and you're just a critic, not a buyer."

"Oh, ho! This is the thanks I get for loaning you my Paris original."

"The thanks you get is that I let you shamelessly abuse your maid's key. If you can afford Paris originals, why can't you afford your own cable TV? What if I'd brought someone home? Even in this city, the sight of a half-naked man on my couch, in my negligee, is enough to make anyone think twice about staying around too long."

"If I had cable, I couldn't afford Paris originals," Doan neatly neutralized her arguments. "And you'd never bring a man here."

"Oh, no?"

"No. You'd rather die than have one of your discards actually . . ." he clutched his breast in mock horror, "know where you live and thus . . . be able to see you again! Oh, stars!"

"So I'm not a romantic. I'm not a cynic, either. Leave me be."

"But," he protested, "if I left you be, I would have no fun at all!"

"Guess what I got in the mail today?" she asked him.

"Your trust check," he answered.

She ran out of the bedroom. "How did you know?"

"Remember? No, of course not. Part of my maid job is to do things that you forget. Like get the mail. When the return address is capped with six last names in scrolly-looking type, it's the family solicitors."

"That could have been anything. I could have all kinds of other dealings with lawyers."

"Yes, that's true. That's why I opened it to make sure. You know, Binky dear, I do love you because you are so much a girl after my own heart, but maybe in this case you are too much after my own heart. If you didn't spend those checks so fast, you wouldn't have to work for a living."

"I'd have to work anyway," she countered. "First of all, because I have no real talents other than clever conversation, which leaves me either very bored or doing good works, and if I'd wanted to be doing good works, I never would've left Connecticut. So first, I work for something to do. Second, if I didn't work, I'd never see any new people and we'd have no one to gossip about."

Doan paled at the very thought of a human life devoid of gossip.

"Also, it would deprive you of men to sink your hooks into."

"Hooks! The nerve. Speaking of which, I really do have to go. . . ." He pulled off the negligee and pulled on a sleeveless black dress.

"Homewrecker. Come see me tomorrow. Saturdays are so dull."

"I'd love to, but I have to leave the country."

"Give me a break. Come over around ten."

"I'll call you when I get back to America!" Doan insisted.

"Get out," she said, pushing him out the door. "I'll see you tomorrow."

Doan shrugged. "Whatever you say, dear."

Detective Luke Faraglione, SFPD, Homicide, did not, to the discerning eyes about him, look like a policeman. At six feet four inches, with black hair and blue eyes, dressed as he still was in his tuxedo, he looked like a model. A self-described Situationist at the front of the roped-off crowd at the mouth of the alley decided that Luke had been sent from central casting to play the bad cop, because good cops were always men who looked like Gene Hackman, or Charles Durning, "or someone else you could never sleep with in a million years," the Situationist drawled.

The Situationist left the scene of the crime momentarily to fetch his video camera. Luke let him go, as Sergeant Connors already had that name down on his pad as a witness to be interviewed later. Detective Luke Faraglione, SFPD, Homicide, did not, today, feel like a policeman. He certainly did not feel like a model. He felt like spending two weeks in the Caribbean, which he would have been able to do in a few days, if it hadn't been for this new killing.

The Situationist was back, filming everything, having decided that if he got it all filmed before anyone realized that this was a real murder investigation, he could claim the whole thing—including tomorrow's headlines—was his performance art piece. He might even be able to get an NEA grant for it.

"Because I could not stop for death," he drawled, training his camera in for a close-up of the dead man, "he kindly stopped for me. The carriage held but just myself, and my nineteen-inch TVs."

Luke shook his head. "Sergeant, would you escort this gentleman back onto the other side of the ropes, thank you very much."

"The victim," the coroner's assistant was speaking into his tape recorder, "is a Caucasian male, twenty-six, with green eyes and . . . well, green hair. The victim is strapped in a position resembling crucifixion to a wall of twenty color television sets, which are attached to twenty videocassette recorders, all hooked to a generator at the end of the alley, all of which were on at the time the body was discovered. The televisions and VCRs do not, at this time, seem to have been all or part of the cause of death," he ended with his usual caution. One never knew.

The top five monitors, Luke noticed, had gone over to snow. When he had arrived several hours ago, they had spelled out, with one word each, "HE DIED FOR YOUR SINS." The rest of the monitors had all played the same thing, each about thirty seconds off the rest—a tape of the dead man's interviews, "performances," lectures, etc. He wondered who would pop for twenty color TVs and as many VCRs for effect, rather than just killing the man. The killer seemed to be not only a certifiable psychotic, but a fairly well-off one.

"This is," a shrill voice in the crowd announced, bringing the rest of them to an awed hush, "the ultimate statement." The crowd parted to reveal an incredibly portly man with a rakish hat and a cloak over his shoulders.

"Oooohhh . . ."

"The ultimate impertinence."

"Aaaahhh . . ."

"The ultimate rebellion against two-dimensional, yes, even three-dimensional limitations of art."

"Mmmmmmm . . ."

"It is . . . the artist . . . *as critic!* The suicide as statement raised to its ultimate level!"

"Oh, what a load of crap," a dour voice interrupted. "This is just the SoMa Killer again."

Luke signaled the already overextended Connors. "That guy. Go get him, will you?"

"I seek in my work," one of the monitors was droning, "to reconcile the Hegelian world with the Freudian, incorporating Socialist Realism, for the full effect I'm, uh . . . looking for."

"Did having rich parents to support you help you in your early years?" an interviewer asked.

"No, it made it harder, because I was too, uh . . . material in my works. I was looking to create something, uh . . . ethereal . . ."

"Don't listen to that!" the man warned Luke.

"Your brain will try and understand it, as if it made sense, and that's the last thing it is."

Luke extended his hand and introduced himself.

"Anthony Chamberlain, art critic, *San Francisco Times*. And always glad to be of help to the authorities. At least, now that I'm on the right side of the law."

"You don't look like the criminal type," Luke told the well-built, ruddy man before him.

"Family business was illegal," he said blithely. "Smuggling artifacts and such out of Indonesia before the Vietnam War. So you could say I was raised around art, and when the business went . . . er, bust, I used it to my advantage."

"So now you're an art critic."

"Yes, one of the last true real critics," he said with characteristic immodesty, "one who can't be bulled into calling trash great art."

"I heard your . . . opinion back there, and wondered if I could ask you a few questions."

"Be my guest." Chamberlain responded.

"From the looks of this, it's our SoMa Killer again. You've obviously already heard of him. This is the third killing of its kind. The victim is always a local artist, always left in the middle of some sort of . . . artwork," Luke said, for lack of a better description. "The first one was impaled on a painting of sorts, which was composed of long shards of broken glass and pottery glued onto a canvas. The second victim had been sealed in plaster and left with some papier-mâché figures sitting on a park bench. And this one, well, I'd say from the look of him that he died by electrocution. Each one of the victims, according to people we've spoken to, who are supposedly experts in the field . . ."

"Hmph."

". . . has been killed and left as part of a work by one school of art or another. Rather than have to ask one of these experts, seeing as how most of them are like that gentleman you had words with, I was wondering if *you* could tell me offhand if you know, first off, how this one would be classified."

"Performance art. All those televisions, for starters. And it's not unusual anymore for artists to crucify themselves as part of a work. Pity the effect is not as permanent in other cases as it seems to be here."

"And is there any artist you know of who . . . works in all three styles that have been instrumental in the murders?"

"All three? Lord, no. They'd rather die than do that. Once you've got your reputation, it's a reputation for doing one thing, one way. Change it, and you'll lose your profitable client base. You know, it sounds awfully silly to declare the death of art; it's just what people did when the most brilliant modern artists came along and shocked everyone out of their complacency. But what comes out as art today is not exploration—it's exploitation. Find a gimmick, and be quick with it. Now, if you ask me, just maybe, there's some poor representational painter out there—maybe even some brilliant modernist whose work really holds some meaning, with reference points outside the Sunday comics and prime-time TV. He'll never make it, you know; his time is past. Not because representationalism or even modernism are bankrupt or no longer speak to us, but because references to comics and TV are the only references anybody gets anymore, and because those other forms are, well, just out of style. Out of style! As if art was as disposable as last year's cocktail dress. Hearing your genuine talent called outdated is certainly enough to make anyone go mad. I'm lucky; I'm a critic with an audience. But if I had nobody to listen to me, well, the temptation to just start offing those commercial bastards would be immense."

"So, in your opinion, we're looking for either a frustrated artist . . . or an angry critic."

Chamberlain laughed. "That sounds about right."

"Thank you, Mr. Chamberlain. You've just saved me from a session with another of our art experts."

"Always a pleasure to save a soul, Detective, from such a horror as that. Good luck!"

Luke sighed as they lowered the body and began disconnecting the electronics from the portable generator. He let his thoughts turn to the Caribbean. Who owes me, he thought idly, so much that I can dump this case on him? A year or two ago, he would have recoiled in horror at the idea that he should give up a case to someone else. But a year or two ago, he reflected, he was a plain old cop, the kind that got vacations. He was hoping with all his heart that a long one now would recharge his batteries enough to get him through until his promotion board came up, and he could send someone else to wade through all this crap.

"What do we do with these TVs, Detective?"

Luke thought a moment. "Turn them all over to *General Hospital*? It's your opportunity to become an artist, Sergeant. Make a statement."

Doan was not happy.

There was a note from Mark on the door. "Roy has forgiven all, I am on my way home, thanx for the couch."

"No problem," Doan murmured as he let himself into the apartment. "I can't be bothered with anyone who won't bother to spell *thanks* correctly, anyway."

On top of that, there was a message from Binky on his answering machine. "You might not want to come over tomorrow, as KC will be here. Unless you can tolerate his presence in exchange for a bottle of Perrier Jouet and some napoleons from the Swiss Bakery. Oh, and I talked to Roy; he's coming over to your place to try and patch things up with Mark."

"I have my own champagne," he said petulantly to the machine, "and I think I'll drink it now." But it was gone from the fridge. "Of course. Markie-poo and hubby making up . . . with my champagne. Probably in my bed, too, for that matter." Sure enough, not only were the sheets hopelessly tangled, but a condom wrapper had been carelessly left on the table by the bed. Doan did not attempt at this time to see if its contents had also been carelessly left behind. "Life," he announced, "is conspiring against me." He sighed heavily, contented himself with a glass of cheap white wine and a Twinkie, and packed for his trip.

Doan's world tour might have fazed other, less experienced travelers, but Doan had already seen such pedestrian destinations as London, Geneva, and Paris, where he was headed now. In his youth, he had not been averse either to men's clothing or men's attentions. His lithe, feline beauty had purchased him more expensive vacations than most people have in their lifetimes. He had trod the Great Wall of China with a billionaire, climbed the Great Pyramid with a fusty Egyptologist, puttered around the Uffizi Gallery with an old WASP, and sailed the seven seas with as many men, all before he was old enough to drink. For Doan, the joy of this trip was not the sightseeing, but the travel—his first chance to ride the Concorde, thoughtfully booked by Eleanor for his convenience.

London occupied him for only a day. Like any good American, Doan was hopelessly enamored of British royalty. However, when one has already met Margaret, Anne, *and* Diana, the changing of the guard seems just a little, well, unimpressive.

Geneva was well prepared for Doan. A town that's

seen everybody from Nazis to Arab sheiks depositing trillions of dollars was not a town to be fazed by a man in a dress. The highlight of Geneva for Doan was that it was smack in the middle of the land of chocolate. It was not his usual habit to make three meals a day of yummy chockie, but then, neither was it his usual habit to visit Switzerland.

Groaning out of his bed the next morning, Doan was not prepared for Paris. Yes, yes, it's a beautiful fossil of a city, a living monument to itself, full of treasures etc., etc. The problem with Paris, in Doan's mind, was that it was always full of Parisians. With the exception of his time in the bank giving over the envelope and instructions, very carefully and slowly in English, he spent his three hours in Paris with his Walkman headphones clamped firmly on his ears to avoid the sound of spoken French and the evil effect it had on his nerves.

Collapsing on the Concorde that third night, he thought it was a very cosmopolitan sort of thing he had done, whipping around the world without stopping to ogle anything, as if he made such a trip all the time. Still, he was glad it was over, and he decided he would stay in Bermuda recuperating until Eleanor's travel expense money was quite exhausted. The possibility of danger to life and limb that Eleanor had hinted darkly at had demolished all his guilt about taking the money. It was, after all, hazard pay. And, he decided, if he was feeling generous, he might even give Binky a call sometime before he returned.

There was no doubt that Doan had had a greater effect on the world's capitals than they had had on him. While he had been singularly unmoved by all those monuments to the long-dead, the living denizens of those cities has been singularly moved by him. Even in Paris, the sight of a man wearing a bright blue silk dress with a wide-brimmed red hat walking into a bank and depositing papers as an agent of a world-famous multimillionairess caused a bit of consternation.

However, Doan had long ago ceased to notice whether or not people were looking at him. He merely took it for granted that they were. This was probably why he had never noticed the man who now sat two rows behind him on the plane, who had been behind him for the last three days. But, then again, the man had been trained to be invisible.

Doan might not even have been perturbed if he'd known he was being followed. He would have immediately felt less like a delivery boy and more like Mata Hari. He might not even have cared if he'd known the man had followed him all the way to sunny Bermuda.

However, he probably would have been upset if he'd known the man checked into the same hotel he did, requested a room on the same floor, and followed him yet again to the offices of the Bank of Bermuda.

And he probably would have been at least a little frightened if he had known that man had, at every one of Doan's stops, waited until a few minutes after Doan had left each bank before going in, explaining to the manager with a smile about eccentric cousin Doan, you can see from that dress of his that he's crazy, he's gone and taken papers from Mother's desk again and left the house, which he's not supposed to do, with those papers, and could I get those back, please, here's a letter from Mother, yes, that's Doan's aunt, he forged her signature on that document he showed you, would you, thanks.

So, by the time Doan (in a man's bathing suit, mind you) spread out his towel by the pool, congratulating himself on a dull job well done, all four sets of the copies of the damning evidence were in the possession of Charles Ambermere's henchman, leaving only Eleanor's originals, deposited in a bank in San Francisco known only to her.

"Ho, ho," Doan chuckled to himself, "his goose is cooked now." And he amused himself watching all the handsome young men dive into the pool until the rhythm of the waves and the song of the breezes in the palm trees rocked him into a light slumber.

"Excuse me," the deep, silky voice said, matching it with a warm, silky touch on Doan's shoulders. "Excuse me."

Doan came out of sleep reluctantly. Opening his eyes, he was satisfied that the vision of male perfection before him was part of another dream, and he promptly started to drift back off.

"Hey! You're already red."

Doan woke up. "Oh my god you're real," he said. Luke laughed. "Yeah, and you're burned."

"I am? But I haven't been . . . oh, that's right. I went to sleep, didn't I? Damn jet lag straight to hell."

"Come on, I've got just the thing in my room."

I bet you do, Doan thought, completely unable to believe his great good fortune.

In his room, Luke Faraglione said, "Lie down on the bed." Doan was obediently there in seconds. "My mom's a nurse, she gets this stuff for free at the hospital."

"Ow. *Ow!*" Doan protested as Luke began to rub the salve into his back.

"Ow. Mm. Mmmm. Aaaaahhhhh. . . ."

"It's Silvodine, they use it on real burns. This stuff works wonders."

"Mmmmmm. . . ."

"Umm . . ."

"Yes?"

"I just think you should know I'm not gay."

Doan said nothing for a moment. "No more salve for me. I want to die. There's nothing left to live for in this malevolent universe of ours."

"Sorry."

"Not your fault," Doan consoled him. "Genetics."

Luke scooped some more Silvodine out of the jar and started massaging it into Doan's skin again.

"But that still feels heavenly. Thank you for waking me before it got too bad."

"Always glad to help a fellow San Franciscan."

"How'd you know that?"

"Saw you check in."

"So?"

"Where else will you find Americans in dresses?"

"Thank you for not saying drag queen, which is something I am not."

"No problem."

"What do you do back home?"

"Cop."

Doan cursed his unlucky stars yet again: friendly, gorgeous, a man in uniform, and straight. This, after all, was Doan's dark secret: in a city where it is not only acceptable but expected that one be unusual, to the point where everybody has a spike rammed through their face to show how different they are from everyone else (save, of course, the several thousand other people with spikes rammed through their faces to prove their individuality), Doan lusted after the conventional. In a city where it was fashionable (and not always difficult) to hate police officers, Doan lusted after them with a passion. There was something about their workmanlike normality that appealed to him; he, after all, was interesting enough for two already.

"And what do you do?"

"As little as possible."

Luke laughed. "You'll have to teach me how I can get that job."

"It requires a certain, well . . . devil-may-care attitude, really."

"Ah. Afraid I never had one of those," Luke said, somewhat surprised to find himself envious of his new friend. "By the way, I'm Luke."

"Doan."

"Dinner tonight okay with you? I came alone."

"So did I. That sounds wonderful." Considering that every man here is after parts I do not possess, he thought, the least I can do is nab someone halfway amusing to talk to. He got up off the bed and examined his back in the mirror. "It looks like several thousand snails have had a hoedown on my back. Yecch, how long does this stay on?"

"Until it all sinks in. Wear real loose dresses for a few days."

"Thank you, I'll do that. Well . . . see you downstairs around six?"

"Yeah. See you then."

Doan called Binky as soon as he got back to his room.

"Hello?"

"Hi, it's me. I'm in Bermuda."

"You lying sack of crap, where are you? Where have you been? I've been calling you for days."

"I told you. Out of the country. Right now I'm in Bermuda. I fell asleep by the pool, and was rescued by a knight in shining armor, who turned out to be straight. Go figure."

"Wait a minute. What are you doing in Bermuda?"

"Running the last of my transcontinental errands for Eleanor Ambermere."

"Oh, come on, Doan, I was starting to worry about you. What's this all about?"

"Come down here and see. She gave me ten grand in expense money. And you've got to see this guy. He is perfect! He's . . . ohhhhh, my God!"

"What? What?"

"Binky?"

"Yes?"

"How many six foot four, black-haired, blue-eyed policemen do you think there could be in San Francisco?"

"What's his name?" she demanded.

"Luke."

"Oh my God, you are in Bermuda, you do work for Eleanor Ambermere, Luke the most gorgeous man in the universe is there with you, and I can't find the gin," she concluded with a scream, rattling madly through the refrigerator until she found the bottle.

"Wanna come down? I'll pay your way."

"But my job . . ."

"Oh, when was the last time you cared whether you got fired or not? You can afford to get fired."

Binky thought about it for all of ten more seconds before she said, "Yes, okay, I'll be there tomorrow."

"Oh, goody! What fun!"

There were all sorts of advantages to wearing dresses, Doan thought as he and Luke followed the waiter to their table. One of them is that it's a hell of a character barometer of the man with you. If he's not

61

embarrassed to be seen with you, he's got more self-assurance than most.

There were few traits in a man Doan prized more than that, and Luke had all of them, too. Few of the diners would ever forget the sight of the tall, dark, gorgeous man in the white suit accompanying the tall, fair man in the white silk dress (neatly accessorized with a black belt).

"Oh, by the way," Doan said casually as he buttered a roll, "I invited someone you know to come down tomorrow."

Luke looked up from the menu. "Oh?"

"You met her at the Policeman's Ball."

"The girl with her head stuck in the floral arrangement?"

"What!" Doan cackled. "Oh, tell, tell!"

"We're talking about Binky, right?"

"That's right. She didn't tell me this part."

Luke entertained Doan with the full account of that evening's events, and Doan proved to be a most appreciative audience, nearly choking on his roll in his glee over the story.

"Well. Will I ever have words for her when I see her. The very nerve of her, not telling me such a story!"

"It is a little embarrassing," Luke said in her defense.

"When I think of all the embarrassing things that have happened to me, and the way I went running to her with the details, I could scream. Could I get another margarita, please?" he asked the passing waiter. "Oh, crap," he said, remembering Eleanor Ambermere. "I'll be back, I have to go make a phone call."

He found a phone and dialed her number. "What," Frannie asked.

"It's Doan. Would you tell Eleanor all the sets are delivered, and I'll be in Bermuda if she needs me?"

"Right," Frannie said, hanging up.

Doan returned to the table. "There. Now, what did she say when you had her all the way out of the flowers?"

THREE

❧

$\mathcal{B}$INKY ARRIVED THE NEXT AFTERNOON, MUCH TO DOAN'S consternation. Her timing meant that he had to meet her while Luke was on the beach, in his tiny black bathing suit that concealed almost none of that massive, gorgeous body . . . alone and unguarded. Doan had decided that if he couldn't have Luke, then Binky had to. Who else would tell him all the details, and wasn't a vicarious night with someone like Luke better than nothing at all?

She was dressed, Doan thought, entirely inappropriately for the task at hand, and telling her so formed his greeting. "You will never, except in Iran and certain parts of Greece and Sicily, attract a man by wearing a black coverall dress. Aren't you already hotter than hell?"

She pushed her sunglasses down so she could eye him over their rims. "In a place where everyone is wearing white, even you, what is more arresting than a woman in black? Besides, it's linen, and I haven't a thing on underneath. I feel fine."

Doan harumphed and led her to a cab. As soon as they were on their way, Binky turned to him. "Okay. Now tell me, what's this about transcontinental errands?"

"Oh, that," Doan said, dismissing his trip abroad (a trip less blithe souls would have killed to take) with a wave of his hand. "Eleanor believes, and I'm afraid justifiably so, that Charles Ambermere would kill her if he knew how much she knew about his recent activities."

"He's such a shit," Binky opined, echoing the opinion of several thousand San Francisco residents.

"Yes, indeedy." He gave her a rundown on the papers.

"Oh, Doan, why doesn't she go to the police?"

Doan looked out at the late-afternoon scene. The beach was sparsely populated, the palm trees waved gently, the sun would not be setting for many hours, but it was already marshaling colors from all the ports of the world in preparation for what was here a daily spectacle. He remembered it had been that way in Tahiti, as well, and he remembered the ecstatic look on the old lady's face when she saw her first tropical sunset. Charles had taken away her money right after that, and it must have seemed to her at the time that she would never see another sunset like that again.

"What she has in mind," he finally said, "is, I'm sure, far more just that anything our judicial system could mete out to him. But don't repeat that to Luke. I don't want to get on his bad side."

"You two seem to have hit it off fairly well, considering how embarrassed you must have felt when you found out he was straight."

"What ever do you mean?" he asked obliquely.

"Oh, come on, Doan. It's me, Binky, and I've seen him. There's no doubt in my mind that you tried to jump him." She laughed. "I bet you felt like dying when he told you. What complete, utter embarrassment."

"Mmmm, yes, dear, it was complete, utter embarrassment. But he was a gentleman about it; he put me quite at ease." He examined his nails, enjoying the circle before the kill. "Probably the same way he put you at ease in that completely, utterly embarrassing moment when he pulled you out of that giant bouquet."

Her eyes widened, but her instincts reacted before her mind, and she only murmured a small agreeing noise.

Doan watched the landscape go by with a smile on his face, thinking maybe it wasn't such a malevolent universe after all.

He didn't let Binky unpack or even rest a minute, so fearful was he that Luke had been nabbed and held for sex. A fruitless search ensued, ending when they got to the hotel pool, where, right before their eyes, two large, capable hands grabbed the concrete edge of the pool, and a pair of arms rippled as they hoisted an incredible expanse of hairy-chested, already-tan muscle out of the water, the head thrown back to make an arc of water off his hair, then one leg, with a thigh almost as wide as Doan's waist, came up and rested on the edge, and then the other, and Luke stood up, dripping water like some primal being from the depths of Binky's libido, and she swooned.

Luke dashed forward and caught her, and when she looked up, she thanked the spiteful urge that had led her to wear black. "You shouldn't wear black," Luke said. "Absorbs too much heat."

At the mention of too much heat, Doan let out a small noise and sat down.

"You're absolutely right," she said, deciding that she would throw feminism to the winds and agree with whatever he said for the rest of her mortal life.

"Why don't we get you upstairs and changed into . . ."

"Something more comfortable?" she interrupted hopefully.

Luke smiled. "Yeah. Something more comfortable."

Satisfaction was not a word Binky used often. There was always something better around the corner, it seemed. She often thought of a line from an Eve Babitz novel, in which dissatisfaction was described as knowing that somewhere there was a fabulous party going on, to which you were not invited. Even the best of pastries, the finest champagnes, the most absolutely fabulous freshly purchased outfit, could only dull the ache of ennui temporarily.

However, at this particular moment, lying in bed with Luke Faraglione after a marathon lovemaking session, Binky knew satisfaction. More, she knew at last what it was like to be in bed with a man after sex and not want him to turn into a pizza. She stretched lazily, writhing like a cat while waiting for Luke to come back from the bathroom. The amount of pleasure she took in watching him cross back to the bed, in all his exquisite buff nakedness, was probably illegal in most Southern states.

"I have never," she stated with authority, "had a lay like that in my life."

"Oh, really?" he asked with a wicked grin. "That's not what Doan tells me."

"What!"

"He says you have a weakness for cops."

She sighed. "I'll kill him. Yeah, it's true, I do. I don't know why. Cops are usually so dull and conservative and humorless . . ."

"The exact opposite of you and your friends."

"That's probably it. I'm so amoral, I guess I like the idea of someone with clear-cut values. I'd never marry one, though, and have to move to the suburbs and be . . . I don't mean I wouldn't marry *you*," she said hastily. "I mean, I'm not saying I *would*, but I

mean . . . oh, shit." Binky hated emotional en-
tanglements; they so often required one to explain
oneself thoroughly, which her upbringing had not
trained her to do.

"I know what you mean. You don't want to end up
married to some meaty-faced guy who wants you to
stay home with the kids except when you're going to
church or the supermarket. I know the kind of cops
you're talking about. I'm not that kind of man."

"Oh, I can tell. That's why I came down here."

Luke raised an eyebrow. "You didn't come down
here for the free vacation?"

She laughed. "As you've probably found out by
now, Doan can be very persuasive."

He laughed as well. "He nearly persuaded me to go
gay."

She idly ran her hands over Luke's buff, hairy
chest. "So how did you become a detective?"

"My father was a cop, and his father, too. The
usual Italian story."

"I thought that was the usual Irish story."

"Same difference."

"And now you're after the SoMa Killer."

Luke sighed. "Not right now, I'm not. I managed
to get off the case."

"Burnt out?"

"No. Yes. The investigation just isn't going anywhere. Nobody seems to have a clue who's bumping
off the worst artists in town, and nobody seems to

care but the cops. And sometimes I think we don't care much, either."

"You mean that being the conservative, bourgeouis type of guys cops are, that the deaths of a bunch of probably Commie pinko faggot artists living off the public teat in the form of NEA grants, isn't exactly a public tragedy?"

Luke sighed. "Something like that. Everybody seems to think it's a big joke."

Binky tactfully decided not to mention that she saw the humor in it, herself. "Everybody except you."

Luke shrugged. "Murder is murder. I guess at heart I am one of those boring, straight-arrow clear-sense-of-right-and-wrong cops you're so attracted to."

"Am I ever," Binky said, terminating the conversation with a carefully placed hand.

Doan saw little of them for the next few days, but that, he decided quickly, was for the best. He'd cased the bars and beaches, searching for someone to help him pass the long, tropical days, but after Luke, every man seemed a bit pale. He was glad when the end of the week came and he was able to extract them from Binky's room.

"Are you mad at me?" Binky asked him in the lounge at the airport, while Luke was away seeing to tickets and seating and luggage and whatnot.

"Mad at you? For snaring Luke?"

"No. For leaving you all alone. You don't look like you had a good time."

"I didn't," he freely confessed. "I spent a day in England, one in France, and one in Switzerland, raced down here, fell asleep by the pool and burned the hell out of myself, fell madly in love with Luke, called you to come down so the three of us could have fun, and then spent three days waiting for you to come out of your room. I definitely need a rest after this vacation's all over. It's been far more trying than I thought it'd be."

"Well, at least you've got ten thousand bucks."

"Oh, look, is that our plane?" Doan asked, getting up.

Binky was immediately alerted. Doan loved gossip, sex, champagne, food, and especially money, which allowed him to enjoy all the others unburdened of a responsible job, and it was not at all like him to gloss over ten thousand dollars, unless . . .

"So," she said. "How much is left?"

"About six hundred," he replied blithely.

"Doan!" She got up, pushed him into his seat, and hovered over him. "*How did you spend nine thousand dollars in a week?*"

"Simple. Our rooms were two fifty a night, apiece. That's a thousand each, so that's two thousand, and I was here a night before you were, that's another two fifty, then there was room service for you and Luke for three days, that's seven fifty . . ."

"Oh, no. That can't be right. We didn't eat that much."

Doan smiled. "I'm sure you didn't, dear. However,

to give you an idea of what we're talking about, your morning pot of coffee cost seven dollars and fifty cents."

"For that little thing? There were only two cups in each one!"

"Oh, is that why you had four each morning?"

"Oh, Doan, I'm sorry, I had no idea. I promise I'll pay you back, I will, really."

"Oh, don't worry about it. I spent more on me than on you, anyway, and it would have been a mortal sin for me to have shattered your paradise with information about how much you were spending. Besides, the bar bill for myself and the dim but incredibly beefy thing I adopted was five hundred bucks by itself."

"But now it's all gone! You could have lived on that for ages."

"Oh, no, that wouldn't have been right at all. It was given to me as spending money, so I spent it. When I'm old and poor and living on cat food, I'll have a memory of a time of complete frivolity to look back upon, a few days where worries about money never entered my head."

"You're not going to live on cat food; I'll feed you if necessary."

"No, I'm not. I'm going to abandon the whole idea of love and marry this doctor who's had his eye on me as soon as we get back. They have buckets of money, and they're never home. It's just like being single and rich! See, I was right. That is our plane. Let's go."

• • •

The first day she was gone, KC had called Binky and gotten her answering machine. "Hi," the recording said, "don't ask me how or why, but I'm on my way to Bermuda for a while. Name, number, blah blah blah . . . you've got one of these, too; you know the drill." He instantly saw Doan's hand in this and decided against leaving a message. He knew that no matter what he decided to say into that machine, it would come out sounding stodgy, repressed, and critical, and would only give Doan more ammunition in his war to make Binky as irresponsible as he was. Even when she'd called him last night, telling him they were on their way back and could he pick them up at the airport this morning, he'd only said, "No problem," and asked her if she'd had fun.

No, he'd leave worse enough alone, wouldn't say anything. He knew Doan thought little of him and the life he led. He often wondered how Binky ended up with two friends so different. While Doan spent his days lunching with heiresses, having tea with people like Eleanor Ambermere, and maybe dusting off a table at Binky's before settling down on her couch for a long gossip session, KC spent his days in his home office getting ready for tax season, when he made the majority of his yearly income. While Doan ate out every night, KC had friends over for dinner at least once a week and took pride in his culinary skills. Doan danced all night for exercise, KC went to the gym and ran each morning. Doan had champagne and pastry for breakfast at noon, KC drank protein shakes for breakfast at the crack of dawn. Doan lived for nightclubs; KC visited bars in the afternoon only to see his friends who were bartenders and left long before the crowds arrived. Doan lived for new import dance singles; KC listened to classical and jazz.

For all his scorn for things peaceful and calm, still, there was something about Doan that . . . no, not attracted him, he dismissed that thought with a laugh. But there were times when he was with him that he felt like he was forgetting to breathe. There was never a lack of excitement around Doan. KC laughed, thinking of what a scene it would be if his friend Stan met Doan. Stan could keep KC laughing for days with his mimicry, and he considered introducing the two of them, if only because Stan's mimicking of Doan would be so . . .

Hell, he thought, I told Stan yesterday that I'd take him down to San Mateo today. He occasionally cursed—but usually accepted—that commandment of city living that said, "He who has a car in the city will always have friends among the nine out of ten who don't." Wait—the airport's right there, right? Drop Stan off, pick them up, no problem.

He smiled to himself. Boring or not, there's a lot to be said for a life where this is the biggest problem I'll have to face today.

KC had obviously not heard of the phrase *Don't tempt fate* when he had spoken. First Stan was late, then they got caught in a traffic jam, and so Binky and Doan's plane was landing as they were passing the airport on their way to San Mateo.

"Uh, do you mind if we get them now?" he asked Stan. "I thought I'd be on time, and, well, they're not the sort of people you want to keep waiting long. Besides, I think you'll get a real laugh out of Doan."

"No problem," Stan had assented.

And it wasn't a problem, at least not until Doan emerged from the plane in an Alexis Carrington-esque outfit, chattering madly to Binky, who was murmuring her inattentive agreements while completely fascinated with every word coming out of the incredibly good-looking man she was arm in arm with. Doan threw his hands up in the air, left them in their mutual raptures, and approached KC—or rather, swept past KC, pulling him into his wake.

"Hello, thank you so much for coming to get us, here's our luggage tickets, Luke was handling all that but he's got to get back to the city as soon as possible, he's the detective investigating the SoMa killings, isn't that fascinating, and Bermuda was so wonderful and I'm sure Binky will tell you all about it when we get back to the city and I would myself, but I've got far too many people to see and things to do that I left behind in my rush to get out of town, and they're all waiting for my attention, and did you see that guy with all the hair back there, he'd be awfully attractive if he'd only do something with that mop, don't you think?" he finished only when he ran out of breath.

He'd turned around to make sure KC was still with him and that Binky and Luke weren't too far behind, and now he found himself looking not at KC but into the gorgeous dark brown eyes of the guy with all the hair back there.

"Absolutely," he agreed with Doan with a completely straight face. "It's a shame."

KC caught up with them then. "Doan, this is my friend Stan. Stan, I've told you about Doan."

Doan bristled, mentally jumping into I'll-kill-him mode. But, "I'll bet you have" is all he said with a smile. "How do you do?"

Stan smiled. "Fine. Pleasure to meet you."

So, Doan thought. This is KC's kind of man. Who'd'a thought? The figure before him was about his own height, wiry but not skinny, with high cheekbones and thin, cruel lips. Best of all, set into this cold, cruel face, were the biggest, warmest brown eyes Doan had ever seen. With consummate skill gained from years of cocktail parties, Doan maneuvered next to KC and spoke in a manner that precluded Stan's overhearing. "Where's the man we've all come to expect you to bring home to meet us, someone named Norman who'll be a bureaucrat who wears boxer shorts and granny glasses? This certainly brings you a notch up in my book." Doan turned to Stan with a smile. "So, dear, what is it you do?"

"I'm an artist."

Doan held the smile (another cocktail party skill) and said only, "How nice." And then murmured to

KC, "You're kidding, right? No, you're not. Oh my God, you didn't have our irresponsible selves around to remind you what happens to people like you when they break out of the dull gray routines they were meant for, so one night you flipped," his voice rose, attracting the attention of those around them, "you went out and that first night all you did was buy a chocolate bar, and you had that instead of your six hundred and forty-seven grain goo for dinner. Then the next night you bought something purple, a sweater or a shirt, and later that night you went out to a bar, and you got up on a table and announced that everyone could have their way with you, three at a time . . ." By this time the three of them had stopped cold, but the traffic behind them didn't mind, far more concerned with how this story ended than with where they had to be. ". . . But only about thirty of them took you up on your offer. And then the next day, oh my God, worst of all, you went to a gallery and you bought some modern art! And you met the artist! And you let him stand there and talk, and oh mercy saints and stars, you fell in love with him! Aaah! The universe is collapsing, the universe is collapsing!"

"Police," Luke announced, "coming through." He deftly pulled Doan through the crowd and out of the baggage area. "Next time you do that, you know, the cop on hand might not be as forgiving as me."

Doan looked up into Luke's eyes, batting his

lashes. "I'd never do anything so dangerous if I didn't have my hero so close at hand."

Luke only shook his head and laughed. "See you later, Doan."

"Bye. You take care, now."

Doan watched Luke leave with a sigh, but it was no longer a forlorn one. Gosh, he thought with surprise, my first straight male friend. Who on earth is it safe to seat one of them with at a dinner party? he thought frantically. He tried to picture Luke fending off a Sister of Perpetual Indulgence on one side, a window dresser from Macy's on the other, and a homewrecker across from him trying to play footsie (you just had to invite a homewrecker or it wasn't a good party), but his reverie was interrupted by a call from behind him. He turned to see KC and Binky, obviously cross with him, and Stan, amazingly enough amused, and he smiled sweetly. "Hello, dears. Which way to the car?"

Somewhere between the terminal and the car, Doan discovered that Stan and KC weren't lovers, and Stan decided he didn't need to go to San Mateo after all. KC asked him repeatedly if he was sure, because it was no trouble at all. He had to ask one last time, before he got into the lane that would put them on the freeway back to the city.

"*Yes!*" Doan shouted, his patience exhausted the second time KC had asked. "*He is sure.* He has said so four times. If he now says that no, he isn't sure, I for one will brand him a wishy-washy wimp for the rest of his life."

KC silently made the turnoff toward the city.

"I'd really like you to come by my studio and see some of my work," Stan said to Doan, and KC almost hit the divider. In all the years he'd known Stan, no one but KC and the owner of the gallery where Stan sold his work had been admitted to the studio. Now, after fifteen minutes of acquaintance, Doan was being granted the trust it had taken the others years to attain.

"Oh, no," Doan said, looking out the window. "Most of the artists I like are dead. I can't stand what comes out as art today."

"Neither can I," Stan said, and Doan gave him a little more of his attention. "I mostly do representational work."

"You mean, like, things and people? Do tell!"

KC was quickly lost in the sea of names behind him, but Doan surprised him. He had somehow managed to know the work of every artist Stan spoke of, and spoke knowledgeably of their lives and works. Not that there was any chance of Doan remaining completely serious for too long, though. The first time Stan spilled a bit of dirt on a fellow artist, Doan was hungry for more, and the rest of the trip Stan spent telling him who was and wasn't gay, who was afraid anyone would find out, who had slept with the owner of a gallery to get his first showing, and so on.

After dropping Binky off, they headed to Stan's SoMa studio. Stan was one of those rare people in San Francisco who lived in an artist's loft and who was actually an artist. When he had moved into his "space," as a real estate agent would call it today, he was generally thought weird for wanting to live in a big room with no walls, above an old warehouse. Now, while his art was considered quaintly old-fashioned, he was indisputably considered a real estate prophet for having bought the property when he did. Doan was not unimpressed with financial acumen in others, although (perhaps because) he had so little of it himself.

"What's the upkeep on this place?" Doan asked.

"Doan!" KC chided disbelievingly. "Stan isn't one of your wealthy patrons, you know."

"So?"

"So you can't just ask perfect strangers about their finances."

"Are you a stranger?" Doan asked Stan sweetly.

"Not anymore."

"Are you perfect?"

"That's for you to decide."

KC can hardly be blamed for suddenly feeling like a third wheel at this juncture. "Call me whcn you're done," he huffed, throwing himself down on a sofa to read a magazine.

"So let's see your stuff," Doan said.

"Start right here," Stan replied, indicating a huge canvas behind Doan.

"Goodness!" was Doan's first reaction. Stan had executed a copy of a Fragonard, identical in almost every respect to that eighteenth-century Frenchman's soft-focus paintings of aristocrats at play, but with one glaring difference. Sitting on the garland-entwined swing hanging from the gracefully arced tree, in a magnificent blue silk dress, was a skeleton, grinning as only skulls can grin. Behind the dear departed was another skeleton, dressed in man's finery, pushing the swing. The ground around them was littered with other dead picnickers and even a happily prancing little dog skeleton.

"I love it," Doan whispered. "But I don't understand. It's so weird, it ought to be popular. I mean, I love it, but it *is* weird."

"Weird in the wrong ways," Stan assented. "Too classical for the big galleries, even if it is filled with dead people having fun."

"What else have you got?"

"Well, in my bedroom, I think you'll find a surprise . . ."

Doan lifted his eyebrows. "Double entendre? And you were doing so well."

"Trust me. You'll be surprised."

KC couldn't help overhearing this conversation, and even though Stan shut his bedroom door behind them (the only door in the place), he could hear Doan's startled "Oh!" When neither further exclamations nor the pair of lovebirds were forthcoming, he thought it time to leave.

He soon found himself at home alone in his own bed, trying to figure something out. It was Doan who had caused the scene at the airport, who had embarrassed him before Stan in the car, who had manipulated him into the long detour out to Stan's.

So why is it, he wanted to know, that it's Stan I'm annoyed with? This, he thought, is not good news.

Little in the way of good news greeted the three returnees, either. Binky discovered that she had, indeed, lost her job with the Police Department for failing to show up or call in for a week, and only moments later, she opened a letter from her wizened old trustees at the bank back East informing her that next month's check would be late, so sorry. Doan's night at Stan's had ended with the two of them drinking several bottles of champagne, painting each other, and then rolling around together on a canvas to make the ultimate modern art statement, which they titled "Jeff Koons's Brain."

Returning home, Doan discovered that his remaining six hundred dollars would have to go immediately to Macy's, as he had impulsively and recklessly purchased a black Chanel suit for the trip (it had been too perfect for the trip's air of mystery to pass up), and Macy's had kindly informed their valued customer that he was exactly that amount over his limit. So Binky was forced to lie to KC to get him to sell a few stocks without a lecture, telling him that she'd lost her job over a little misunderstanding and that she'd have another in no time flat. Doan was forced to take a more drastic measure. He had returned to the part-time job in a record store that he'd abandoned, he'd hoped, forever.

But it was Luke who had the worst luck of all. He hadn't unpacked before the call came: The SoMa Killer had struck again, and he was back on the case.

This time, he found out at the scene of the crime, the murderer had merely crushed the artist's head in with a psychedelically painted pipe. All the renewing energy of that week in the Caribbean, all the ecstacy of three days with Binky, was drained from him when a collector approached him at the scene of the crime and asked him if the "work," dead man not included, might possibly be up for sale sometime in the near future.

Then it got worse, as he heard a horribly familiar voice behind him ordering the plainclothesmen, his men, about. He turned around, and there he was, Sergeant Seamus Flaharity, who saw him, shouted his hello, and began working his way across the dead man's studio toward him, destroying evidence with every careless step. "Well, Detective, we've sure got a mess here, eh? This killer's real fond of messes, that's for sure. Not to worry, you've got me on your team now!" Luke said nothing, only looked momentarily to heaven before heading out of the building and away from Flaharity, into his car, and back to the station.

"Don't say a word," Captain Fisher said before he had the door all the way open. "It wasn't my decision."

"Oh, come on, Captain. You could've blocked it. Now I've got that incompetent bastard to deal with. Do you know what he'll do if he even overhears the name of a suspect? He'll find the guy and beat him until he confesses. That's what happened when he got into Marsh's investigation of Sykes. A murder investigation's not like breaking up a street fight."

"It was the chief's own decision."

Luke sat down, deflated. "Shit. Why?"

Captain Fisher blew on her coffee, took a sip, blew again, then took another. It was a delaying tactic that allowed angry subordinates to cool off before she faced them with the mysterious ways that bureaucrats wielded their power over policemen.

"Flaharity is a liability in most parts of this city. So we keep him in the Sunset, where he's a hero. Every now and then he busts some kid's head open, and we move him downtown until the press cools off. The chief can't fire him, can't reprimand him, and can't leave him be. Besides, you know cops: a big killing is a gravy train in overtime, and everybody wants their share of the pie."

"Why not delegate him to paperwork, for Christ's sake?"

"Nope. Too deliberate a slam, and the Irish contingent's still got a lot of say on the force." She smiled. "Have some coffee."

Luke sighed with defeat and accepted the coffee, leaning back in his chair. Maybe Doan was right, he thought. Maybe it was a malevolent universe after all.

Sergeant Flaharity wondered what Connors was up to, staring down at the floor like that, and came over to offer his help. "What do we have here?" he asked, stepping on a piece of paper with a painted footprint that didn't match the dead man's shoes, obliterating it instantly. Connors groaned, put his hands over his face, and left before he struck a fellow policeman.

"Sergeant, over here."

Flaharity began to amble toward the man from the lab, who paled. "Sergeant Connors, hurry!" he said in a panic, fearing that Flaharity would somehow manage to destroy this piece of potential evidence as well.

Connors was no younger than Flaharity, but it wasn't hard to be in better shape, and he handily beat him to the other side of the studio. "Yeah, what've you got?" The lab man handed him a piece of paper in a plastic bag.

Connors examined the prints lifted from the pipe, and then the paper. When he was done, he said, "I think you'd better call Detective Faraglione. Now."

"And then what?" Doan demanded of Binky over the phone, ignoring any potential customers in the record store where he held yet another part-time position.

"Wait a minute." He turned to his coworker in the record store, a fortyish man with granny glasses and a death-defyingly huge head of curly hair. "Could you turn that down a little, please?"

"Heeeeyyyy, maaaannnn! Whutttsss thuuuhh haaasssssle?"

Doan gritted his teeth, smiled, and turned the Dylan record back down to an indiscernible level.

"What's that noise?" Binky asked. "Sounds like someone gave a record contract to a singing rat."

"It's a Bob Dylan album."

"That's what I said."

"Now, what did you two do for three days? Tell!"

"I can't."

"*What?!* What do you mean you can't tell? Why not? What other reason is there for going to bed with someone other than to tell? Well, in his case I can see a good reason, but still! We tell each other everything. Why do you want to stop now, in my hour of greatest need?"

"Because . . . I don't know. It just feels like something private."

"Oh, my," Doan said, watching the old hippie disappear into the back room for a joint. "Is this love?" He turned the volume back up after putting on the *Liquid Sky* soundtrack.

"Maybe. No, it can't be. I don't know!" she finished with a forlorn wail.

Doan sighed. "I know, believe me, I know."

Binky's voice immediately lost its despairing tone. "What?"

"I think I'm in love, too."

"Oh, come on. Stan? Already?"

"Binky, he's just wonderful. He's a great artist, he's so much fun to be with, and that's even when we're out of bed, and in bed . . . well, let me tell you."

"Yeah, yeah, tell me!"

"Can't. It's love."

"Bitch!" she accused.

Doan looked down from his perch at the register at the young lady before him. "No, no, no! A thousand times no!" He snatched the record from her hand. "How many times do I have to say it? I won't sell children Whitney Houston albums! They'll rot your brain. When you're twenty-one and responsible for your own destruction, I'll let you have it. Do your parents know you're getting this shit? And no Michael Bolton, either!" he called after the rapidly retreating innocent.

"Are you having a hard time of it?" Binky asked him.

He shrieked. "You were right, I should have kept some more of that money. All they'll let me wear is a simple print shift, and I have to wear a *name tag!* 'Hello, my name is . . . DOAN!' Get me out of here!" he demanded unreasonably.

He heard a click-click. "Hold on," Binky said.

"Oh, no. I hate that call waiting thing. PG&E is

lucky that I let *them* put me on hold. *You* call me back."

Doan put the phone back in its cradle and removed the *Liquid Sky* soundtrack from the turntable. The music was ideal for aggravating hippies, but after a while it even aggravated Doan. Seeing three heavy metal heads enter the store, he replaced it with a thumping disco Pet Shop Boys mix. He soon had the whole store to himself, so he settled back into his chair to read a book. No sooner had he opened it than the phone rang. "Strawberry Electric Pop-Tart Aquarius Acid Trip Records," he answered.

"Is that really what that place is called?" Binky asked distantly.

"Yes indeed, God help us all," Doan answered, wondering what was so suddenly wrong.

"Oh. Um . . . I have some bad news for you."

"Bad news? Let me guess: You've talked to the owner of this dump, and he's not going to fire me so I can collect unemployment."

"It's Stan."

Doan was instantly alert. "What?"

"He's been arrested."

"For what?"

"Murder."

Doan met Binky and KC at the Hall of Justice. They were engaged in a serious conversation with Luke. *"Where is he?"* Doan demanded. *"Let him out now!"* While Doan's loving frenzy might seem unreasonable to most of us who recall our first few days of knowing someone, let it be recalled that Stan possessed the four qualities that Doan had long ago settled upon as necessary should he ever take a husband: good looks, great sex, dry sense of humor and, while he didn't own a palatial home, Stan's large, airy loft was reasonably fabulous. Besides, gay time is different than straight time—a second date is considered a serious relationship.

Luke took Doan in hand and led him over to the corner where the three of them had been talking. "Your friend's been arrested for murder. There's some evidence that he's the SoMa Killer."

Doan promptly sat down on the floor. "That . . . is impossible."

Luke showed him a copy of the most damaging piece of evidence, the note found in the last victim's studio.

Dear Thief:

Everything you've done you've stolen from someone else. You try and sell that painting and I'll come wrap one of your I beams around your head.

Your victim.

"That's no proof!" Doan shouted.

"I'm afraid that's Stan's handwriting. And Stan's prints are on the murder weapon."

"He picked up an I beam and bashed someone's head in with it?"

"No. It was a pipe. Same general effect, though."

Doan got up, a determined look on his face. He turned to Luke. "How much to bail him out?"

"Well, let's see. He's got no record, but he is a suspected serial killer. Chances are that bail will be denied."

"I want to see him." And he began marching toward the visitors' entrance.

"There's no arguing with him at times like these," Binky told Luke.

Luke sighed. "What the hell. Stan's got no relations. I'll put Doan down as his brother, that'll get him in."

Binky hugged Luke. "You're an angel."

"Tell me more."

"*Darling!*" Doan yelled as he ran toward Stan, but he lost a little of his enthusiasm when he bumped his nose into the glass divider between Stan and himself. Stan pointed to the phone in Doan's visitor's cubicle.

"You sure know a lot about how things work around here." Doan said into the phone. "Come here often?"

"Sure," Stan said bitterly. "I'm always out murdering someone."

"Now, now. You can't lose heart. Can I bring you anything?"

"Yeah, a cake with a shotgun in it for me to use on whoever set me up."

"Hmm. I'd have to make a sheet cake to hide a

shotgun, and those are so trying. Would you settle for a good lawyer?"

"I'd settle for a good reason why I'm here."

"The note, dear."

"What note?"

"The note they found in the studio. From you, telling him that if he sold some painting, you'd kill him. What painting?"

"Oh, crap." Stan leaned back and rubbed his eyes with his free hand. "That. I did this gag sketch, I did it as a joke. I just put every bad artist's device I could think of into it, and I showed it to some dealer at a party who I thought might get a laugh out of it and he . . ." He laughed and shook his head. "He took it seriously. He wanted me to paint it, so he could buy it. Well, he wasn't happy when I told him it was a joke. Anyway, Arbuthnott . . ."

"Beg your pardon?"

"Arbuthnott. My supposed victim's name. He was there, and he obviously overheard me, because the next thing I know, I'm in a gallery looking at this painting, it's from my sketch, and it's got Arbuthnott's signature and a ten thousand dollar price tag on it . . . and it's marked *sold*."

"So you sent the little creature the note."

"Right. That's it."

"Then why, love, are your fingerprints all over his studio?"

Stan flushed. "I didn't exactly send it. I kind

of . . . hand delivered it. Having gotten in through a locked window."

"With a brightly painted pipe."

"Yeah, how'd you . . . oh, shit. I left it there."

"Well. That might explain why the police think you're guilty, all right," Doan said defeatedly.

"Christ, Doan, I appreciate your coming here, really." He smiled his melting smile. "But there's not a whole hell of a lot you can do for me. I mean . . . you're not what anyone would consider a political powerhouse."

Doan looked at him, smiled, then began to laugh. "Oh, if only you knew. If only you knew." He got up. "I promise you, darling, you'll be free in no time."

Doan came out of the jail and dashed past the three of them. "We're going to get Stan off the hook."

"How?" Binky asked.

"Meet me tonight. At Le Club."

Le Club, in spite of its having the most unimaginative name in a city full of imaginatively named nightclubs, was the hottest club in the city; at least, it was when you started reading this paragraph. It was one of the first gay clubs with the foresight to go from disco to new wave, and was again the first to go from there to house. The only way to stay ahead of radio and MTV and the other clubs was to have the best dance music first. And only someone with enough time on his hands to read all the domestic and foreign music magazines and listen to anything that looked interesting—all purchased with Le Club's money—could keep up with the ever-changing music scene and placate the ever-finicky crowds. So Doan McCandler had a job, a real job, mind you, from midnight to 6 A.M. Friday and Saturday nights, a job that suited his personality as he could go to it when and if he felt like it. One weekend he'd gone off to the Russian River with a new gentleman friend, and revenues had been off 50 percent from previous Friday nights, as the regulars heard a top forty song on the speakers, concluded from this that Doan wasn't in the booth, and left. The fact was that Le Club's livelihood depended on its Friday and Saturday night take, and that take depended on Doan McCandler's talent for spying out the newest rage to be—thus the sole reason he had retained this job for six months, the longest he'd ever held one job.

Binky knew Doan was in full form when she saw him standing under the marquee at Le Club. It was already dark when she and KC arrived, and the shadows on the street lent an extra air to the six foot two man in an Indiana Jones hat, sunglasses, and a trenchcoat over his prom dress.

"What's with the secret agent outfit?" KC asked.

"We are marked women. You never know what assassins the Grand Order of the Knights of Cubism have sent after us. Quick, inside!"

They went upstairs to the DJ booth. Doan shrugged out of his trenchcoat, waved to the cheering crowd as the departing DJ announced him, cued up KLF's "Last

Train to Transcentral," and fell into his chair, his headphones accessorized insouciantly around his neck.

"Right-o!" he said, and extracted a piece of paper from his bosom. "I've been working on a few ideas. What do we know so far?" He readied the latest Orb remix on the second turntable. "First of all, that Stan is innocent. We all believe that, yes?" They agreed. "Second, the police have arrested Stan on the flimsiest of evidence." He looked at them, and neither of them dared to say that a threatening note and fingerprints at the scene of the crime were rather incriminating. "Third, what's the best reason for killing an artist? Besides for being awful. Because the works of dead artists are worth more than the works of living artists, right?"

"Luke's looking into that," Binky said defensively. She knew Stan was innocent, even though she'd just met him. After all, he was a friend of KC's, and he and Doan had fallen in love at first sight. What better character references could Stan have in her eyes? All the same, the suggestion that Luke wasn't doing his job irked her. "You know, he didn't want to arrest Stan."

"No," Doan agreed. "But after I cooled down, I called Luke and we had a little chat, and I agreed jail was the best place for Stan."

"What?" "Huh?" Binky and KC asked disbelievingly.

"Well, it's true. Luke has a suspect under arrest, which gets his superiors off his back, so he can do his job. The real killer thinks he's gotten away with murder, so he'll be less careful. And this way, if there's another murder, they'll know Stan's innocent, because he's got the perfect alibi. And that frees us up to use all assets at our disposal."

"All right, Doan," KC said impatiently. "What assets do we have?"

"Our wits. I shall no longer be Cornelia Guest, good-time debutante. I shall now become . . . Nancy Drew!"

"Shit," KC said irritably. "Come off it. Look, one of my best friends is in jail, and you want to play games."

Doan smiled ever so slightly, and Binky, knowing the warning signs, sat down out of the way. "He's become a little more than a friend to me."

KC snorted derisively. "Yeah, I'll bet. Look, he doesn't have any money, he doesn't even have any charge cards, so you might as well start looking in other directions for your new source of support."

"KC!" Binky whispered, horrified.

Doan was still smiling. "It's all right. Really. I'll just call my friend Martin Hart and tell him I won't be needing his services after all. And then . . ."

"Wait a minute," KC said. "Martin Hart?" He refused to believe that Doan could know one of the city's most prominent trial lawyers.

"Yes. He's Stan's new lawyer. Martin owes me a few favors. So I'll call him and cancel that arrangement, and then cancel my appointment with a certain someone for whom I provide, shall we say, a goodly amount of grist for his mill?"

Only in San Francisco would that remark be understood, but in the city, everyone understood. Art Mill's daily column, "Grist for the Mill," had been running for some thirty years, thriving on Mill's ability to discover firsthand, or from a reliable source, exactly what everyone in the city was doing. And he reported every behind-the-scenes going-on of every famous name without ever using the name, merely dropping a hint that would in any other city be too broad, such as "big-time developer," "culture vulture numero uno," "local movie trillionaire." But the readers of the paper knew them all instantly. Visiting out-of-towners were completely baffled by all such references, but that was due to San Francisco's unique character; it was, really, the nation's biggest small town, where some were tolerant and others were bigots, but they were all nosy Parkers, all members of the world's largest and yet most exclusive club.

And Art Mill played no small part in spreading the glue that held the city together. Men who got instant admission into the offices of kings and presidents were kept waiting for Art Mill unless they'd arrived with a juicy tidbit for the column. There was, however, a small list of mostly unknown names, the names of those who were always welcome, and Doan McCandler was on it.

Binky and KC exchanged disbelieving glances.

"Surely you don't doubt?" Doan asked. "But you've

seen my code name in the column hundreds of times: 'The man who sleeps with those who know'?"

"You?" KC accused.

"Oui. Moi. Will one of you go to the bar and get me a pitcher of tonic and ice? Just tell Larry it's for me." Binky, after an examination of the dance floor below, decided KC was most likely to make it through the ecstatic dancers and back without succumbing to the waves of love.

"The man who sleeps with those who know," Binky said accusingly after KC was dispatched. "And all this time, I thought you spent your nights at home yelling at the TV."

"Oh, honey, I don't sleep with all those men. But closet cases tell me the stories of their lives in the hope that I'll give them a tumble, which I don't, and alcoholic matrons take me to lunch and rat on their husbands. And Eleanor hears all sorts of dirt, people are so free with their tongues around her because so many of them think she's still crazy. Free drinks, free food, and Art pays me to boot."

"I don't understand. Le Club pays you. Art Mill pays you. The record store pays you. Eleanor Ambermere pays you. Even I pay you. But it always seems like you're broke and never doing anything."

He indicated what he was wearing. "Do you know you can't buy a black prom dress? You have to have it made to order. And it cost a bundle. And I couldn't be caught out in less than the best. Hand me that Cure record, would you? The orange one."

KC returned with the pitcher and glasses.

"Thank you," Doan said.

"Umm," KC said, looking at the floor. "I'm sorry about what I said earlier. Stan's my friend, and I'm worried about him, that's all."

"No problem," Doan said blithely, dismissing the subject. He filled their glasses and raised his own. "To success!"

"To success!" they echoed.

FOUR

DOAN HAD HIS RESERVATIONS ABOUT SEEING ART MILL. Something had happened to Mill, and Doan didn't know whether to ascribe it to disillusionment, midlife crisis, or something else entirely. But the wisecracking man about town was gone; Mill was no longer the man who cackled over Doan's stories, dropped previously scheduled items to fit the newest dirt in, paid Doan off and sent him on his way with an admonition to "keep 'em talking." The new Mill greeted Doan wearily, got a chuckle out of the stories, and told him he "couldn't use them, sorry, but why doncha siddown and have a cuppa." The new man reflected in the columns, as fewer and fewer of them were about current social events, and more were reminiscences about the old days, and where once the death of an old friend of his was an item, now it was a column. The plight of the homeless consumed the next day, the shabbiness of the city the next, the uglification of the skyline the day after that—that is, when Mill wrote his own column at all; he now had half a dozen assistants writing most of it for him.

The city still loved Art Mill. But sometimes the city wondered if Art loved it as is, or only as it had been. Doan was too young to remember the people and places and things Art reminisced about. But he was old enough to know that today is never the beloved golden age until it's already yesterday. He was hoping Art would help, for Stan's benefit, of course, but also for Art's own—a good dose of adventure, Doan had decided, was exactly what was needed to bring the man back among the living.

"Hello, Doan," Art's secretary greeted him.

"Is Art busy?"

She shook her head. "Staring out the window again. Go wake him up. Hey! What's with the outfit?"

Doan was wearing a man's shirt and pants. He shrugged. "Just too wrapped up in some things to get dressed," he lied, for reasons which will be revealed in their proper place.

"You in pants. That'll wake him up."

Doan entered Art's office, and Art was indeed staring out the window at the depressing area around the newspaper building.

"South of Market," Art said, not turning around to identify his visitor. "Calcutta by the bay. Disgusting. Ball parks get bundles and Glide gets nothing."

"And do you remember, just a few years ago, everyone said it would all be gone, Yuppiefied, sanitized. And it's not! There are little islands of delicious icy sterility, little ziggurat kingdoms of concrete condos, but all the filth all around is still there! It's so reassuring."

Art chuckled and turned around. "Hello, Doan. I wouldn't have lectured if I'd known it was your frivolous self. . . . Oh my God those are . . ."

"Men's clothes. Don't give me a hard time; I don't have the energy to deal with it this morning."

"Oh, yeah? What's going on?"

Doan poured himself a cup of coffee and sat down. "Awful things, with which I need your help."

"Go on."

"A friend of mine's been arrested as the SoMa Killer."

Art perked up. "What? Is he guilty?"

"Art!" Doan protested.

Art threw his hands up. "Sorry. Still, you've always said the SoMa Killer was doing us all a good deed. No offense, but it wouldn't surprise me if you told me he was guilty and you put him up to it."

"Would you turn me in if I did?"

"Are you kidding? I'm getting more mileage out of this thing in my column than I've gotten out of anything since Feinstein's hair. It's a slow news week, kid, get your friend sprung so he can go kill again."

"Well, returning to reality, he's innocent. His name's Stan Parks, he's an artist . . ."

103

". . . And he's being framed?" Art asked with a smile, completely unable to resist a play on words.

"If you do that again, I shall have to kill you," Doan warned him. "But yes, he's been set up. See, the latest one to die was Mortimer Arbuthnott, would you believe they called him a traditionalist because he was still working with I beams? But he stole one of Stan's ideas and made a mint off it." Doan told him about the painting, and Art laughed.

"Is this for real?" he asked.

"Yes. It's rather sad to have to say it, but yes."

"You want that in the column, is that it? I don't think that's going to help get your friend off. It'll sure get him some sympathy, but . . ."

"No . . . that's not exactly what I came for."

"Okay, Doan. You know I owe you a few. Shoot."

Doan eyed him levelly. "You're going to help me find the SoMa Killer."

Art laughed. "Come on, Doan. What the hell am I supposed to do?"

"You're a journalist. Dig for facts. Think, Art. . . . Who wants artists dead? Jealous artists, extremist critics, those I can handle. But what about gallery owners and collectors? I know everyone worth knowing, certainly, but there are a staggering number of people in this city who wouldn't give me the time of day. Jealous of my wardrobe, no doubt. That's where you come in. You can see who sank a lot of money into stuff by the dead men, who might benefit from their sudden death."

Art shook his head. "Why don't you tell this to the cops?"

Doan laughed. "Art, I got all these ideas from a cop. Luke Faraglione is handling the investigation. . . ."

"Oh, the one who nabbed the Belli dognapper?"

"Right. So I just sat there and listened to him tell me what kind of leads he was going to check out. However, he is a policeman, and they do make people nervous. You, my love, are a columnist and a social fixture, and are quite well acquainted with most of those people. You can ask them questions in a manner that won't put them on guard, at least not right away."

Art sighed. "All right, Doan. I'll see what I can find out for your investigation."

"*Our* investigation."

"Right, right."

Doan smiled to himself, knowing Art was hooked.

Binky was in a bad mood. It was as if the fates had decided that her tropical jaunt had been too much fun; she'd exceeded her happiness quota for at least a year, judging from the way things were going now. No job meant no paycheck, which she could live without. That only meant no luxuries for a while. No trust check, however, was a different matter. That meant no necessities: no coffee beans, no weekend pastry, no champagne, no new outfits. So rather than bite the bullet for a month, she had committed what her upbringing had instilled in her was the cardinal sin—she had dipped into capital.

Now she had to go to an art gallery. This was not something she was looking forward to, either, for another childhood lesson had been "if it's in a museum, it's art. If we own it, it's art. If it's for sale in a store, it's trash." To the Van de Kamps, even the most prestigious art galleries were still only stores. This was an attitude that proved useful to her in resisting certain peer pressure at college, where every clench-jawed deb was majoring in art and encouraging her to do the same. They did this not out of any interest in art, but because it would be important in their future careers as Main Line matrons to make people think they were interested in art. Not to mention that there was great social cachet in having an artist at your dinner party, and if you couldn't speak knowledgeably about art, how could you expect to dominate conversation? And how could you be a social lion without at least one museum wing named after yourself?

The Van de Kamps were old money, older money than even Eleanor Ambermere's, and that venerable family looked with slight disdain on the philanthropic ways of the social climbers. Nouveau riche give to museums named after them; old money gives to museums named after their grandfathers.

So Binky had not been expected to absorb too much on the subject, much to her relief. She was so busy not doing all the things she was expected to do that one more thing to not do might well have been the end of her.

But she had been the one chosen to go to the gallery by Doan, who had assumed a military bearing as of late (along with a tendency toward khaki skirts and sailor dresses) to go with his new position as general of the resentful forces of Binky, Luke, and Art Mill.

"Why me?" she had wailed in protest.

"Because," Doan had explained. "You're the only one who can pull it off. KC looks like he has beefcake posters on all his walls, maybe a Remington print in the living room to show his tricks how butch he is, and a Rockwell in the bedroom from his mother. I look like I'm into famous dead female drug addicts, which I most certainly am not, but that's another story. But you, my dear, ooze class and money. People see that jaw shaped like an old-style cash register, and they think that when it opens it's going to spit money everywhere. And that accent you've worked so hard to be rid of? Punch it up a little, and people are your slaves. They despise you, but they're your slaves."

So once more her past had caught up with her, and she found herself in front of Le Gallerie (which, despite appearances, was not owned by the same people who owned Le Club—phony French names were again the rage). On prominent display in the front of the gallery were several paintings by a man famous not for these paintings, but for the fact that he did not paint them; rather, he hired people to paint them for him. Each one was done in the same style, necessarily very simple as to be duplicated by anyone: Casper the Friendly Ghost figures wandering in and out of vague settings, with the whole painting looking more like the sort of thing airbrushed onto the side of a van than anything else.

"It's very gripping, isn't it?" the woman who had appeared at her side asked her.

"It gives me a chill," she said, unable to resist one comment before slipping into character.

"Notice the use of shading, the absence of vibrant color . . ." The saleslady went on in this vein while Binky nodded dutifully in agreement.

"Yes, yes," she said. "Due to the artist's belief that the world is a colorless place."

"Yes!" agreed the saleslady heartily, smiling at Binky the way a professor will smile at a student who has spouted the correct answer.

"I understand," Binky began, "that this gallery represents the late Mr. Arbuthnott."

The saleslady assumed the proper look of mourning. "A terrible tragedy. A shock to us all. So young and talented."

"Indeed. And did he, by chance, make any last deliveries to the gallery for sale before he . . . met his unfortunate end?"

"Oh, yes," she nodded. "Mr. Arbuthnott was most prolific. We received two sculptures and four paintings the week before he died. What is your favorite of his works?"

Binky panicked. A name, a name, she was supposed to know the name of at least one of his works. Grasping onto the most repulsive topic she could think of, she stabbed in the dark. "Sores."

The saleslady lit up. " 'Funeral of Sores'?"

"Yes, that's the one." Good Lord, she thought. "Do you have that one?"

"Oh, no. As a matter of fact, our entire catalog of Mr. Arbuthnott's works were bought out last week."

Binky's interest rose. "Really?"

"Yes, and all by the same customer. Right before . . . the tragedy."

"Ah. And who would that be?"

The saleslady frowned. "I'm sorry. Client information is privileged."

"Oh, yes, of course. So sorry. Does . . . does that happen often, that someone's whole catalog is purchased all at once?"

"Oh, almost never. At least, not while they're alive."

Binky smiled sweetly yet demandingly. "Could you at least tell me, was it a private collector or a museum? If it's a museum, I'd love to view his last works."

"No, I'm sorry. It was a private buyer. Could I interest you in one of our promising new artists . . ." She took Binky by the arm and began leading her toward the back of the gallery.

"Oh, no, so sorry, thank you ever so much, I really

ORLAND OUTLAND

must be going now. You've been a great help. Thank you."

Once outside, she swore Doan would pay for the rest of his natural born days for what she'd just been through, and then she made a beeline for the liquor store.

As it had been easier to lie to Binky about his appointment with Eleanor than to explain the extensively complicated truth, so it was easier for Doan to tell Art he was dressed as a man because he just felt like it than to give the real reason. But, truth be told, Doan never really felt like wearing men's clothes. The fact of the matter was that Doan was going to the Pacific Union Club, none too affectionately known as the PU by many residents, Art Mill included. Mill had been blackballed more than once.

The PU was a fairly unprepossessing—hell, downright ugly—building on Nob Hill, an old San Francisco mansion converted into a gentlemen's club. The house and surrounding lawn (on which nobody had ever been seen doing anything but cutting it) took up nearly a square block in the heart of the luxury hotel district. It was a signal banner of the power and infinite wealth of its members that they held onto this property as if to say that the money to be made from selling a square block of prime real estate wouldn't really impact their financial worth enough to warrant the bother of relocating their club. And *that,* my friends, is *rich.*

San Francisco is a city full of rich people. Rich, rich, rich. There are more rich people per capita in this town than any other in the nation. (We are also proud to be the pedestrian death capital of America!) And not a one of them will ever admit it. "I'm not rich!" a fabulously wealthy woman this author once worked for used to cry, in between calls to her personal banker, her housekeeper, and her fellow board members of her childrens' private school. The PU flew in the face of all that, in typical alpha male fashion. "We are *so damn rich*," the PU trumpeted, "we could kill you and get away with it three times over."

Doan was there to meet a member—nay, the member's member, Martin Hart, celebrity lawyer extraordinaire, who was familiar to millions for his talent for popping up on TV whenever a notorious murder trial took place. Hart was pure San Francisco in the way that San Francisco likes to think of itself: colorful, always in the papers, more than a bit of a rogue, a little shady in his financial dealings . . . the sort of person who, in other cities, is driven out of town on a rail by zealous reformers, but who, in San Francisco, gets elected mayor.

Doan had not rescued Mr. Hart, Esq. from a speeding wheelchair, but had met him in more pedestrian circumstances. To make a long story short, especially since nobody except Hart himself understands how it works, Doan had yet another part-time job appearing as "corespondent" in divorce cases in states without no-fault divorce, in place of some actual corespondent who wished to remain anonymous. When Hart's clients found out that their spouses were putting private eyes on them to build up a good divorce settlement, they hired Hart to hire Doan to make dramatic entrances into hotels with said clients, giving the spouses the ammunition they needed to get the divorce, which the clients secretly wanted, often because they were about to strike it rich and didn't want their imminent fortunes to become community property. Suffice it to say it was all very complicated, and perhaps it would be best to say that Doan worked part time for Martin Hart and leave it at that.

Needless to explain, it was Stan Parks's plight that brought Doan to the PU on a rainy day. Doan was ushered into a small private room with two fat, lazy leather armchairs, one of which was already occupied. "So, Doan," Martin Hart asked silkily, "what criminal activity of yours brings you to see me?"

Doan's eyes widened and he put a hand to his chest. "Oh, it's not for *me*. You know me, Martin—I'd *never* do anything illegal. That I could get caught doing."

Hart laughed. He was one of those people Doan liked in spite of himself. He really should hate Hart, defender of murderers, drug kingpins, and anybody else who would guarantee him a headline. But Doan liked Hart for his blatant disregard of the rules, and he'd learned long ago that sometimes it takes a rule-breaker to get things done—like, for instance, catch another rule-breaker.

"It's about the SoMa Killer," Doan began, but Hart held up a hand.

"Say no more. You wish me to defend Stan Parks on murder charges. I'll do it."

"Of course you will, darling; la publicitee will be huge. That's not what I was going to ask you."

Hart's studiedly bushy white eyebrows lifted. "Oh? Now I'm interested."

"Stan is innocent. I need your help to prove it."

"That's what I do."

"No, I mean *now*. Look, Stan didn't do it. No, seriously! Martin, you know me, you know my instincts about people."

"Hmm. Yes, I do. Go on."

"I need your devious mind to help me. Don't arch those eyebrows at me! You *are* devious and you know it. Help me think who might have a motivation to kill these artists. The police don't care—well, one of them does, but that's another story—because they've got someone under arrest. The papers don't care; 'Jealous Artist Kills Six' is a great headline. But I want your help to think of who else might have done this."

"Is there a personal connection here?" Hart asked tactfully.

"He's my boyfriend," Doan said. "I know, I sound like Cloris Leachman in *Young Frankenstein*. Nobody in authority seems to care about catching the real killer and exonerating Stan, so . . . I'm marshaling my resources."

"Well, Doan, if I know you and your resources, this shouldn't take long. All right." Hart put the tips of his fingers together and made a pyramid under his chin, a device that worked like a charm in court, and which he had thus incorporated into real life, making it all the more natural-looking in court. "We're talking about the art world. I suppose I know about as much about that as anybody outside it. You've got artists, dealers, critics, collectors . . . any other types?"

"Wannabes. Groupies. Assorted hangers-on."

"Your kind of people. You handle that end."

"Hmph!" Doan snorted.

"All right. The cops, bless 'em, have arrested an artist because the killings look like some kind of artistic protest against modern art. Now, I ask you, is that obvious or what? So if it's an artist, it's a frustrated, second-rate one."

"Stan is a genius."

"Fine, fine, for the sake of argument, we will assume nothing I say can possibly apply to Mr. Parks. A critic? I doubt it. Any critic worth his salt can destroy a reputation without lifting a finger. Now, that leaves us with dealers and collectors. Aha! People with a financial interest. Are you following me?"

"Every step."

"Collectors might kill artists to raise the value of their works."

"So might a dealer."

"Very good. It's a little transparent, a little cynical, a little too . . . ridiculous? I like it."

"Sure you do. You approved of the abuse excuse in the Menendez trial."

"We're not just talking about greed here," Hart continued. "We're talking about *desperation*. Someone who needed the profit a dead artist's works would fetch." He leaned back, satisfied with himself. "There you are. Find somebody associated with the dead artists—their dealers, their collectors." He rose up. "Now, if you'll excuse me, the Simpson defense team is calling."

"Et tu, Brute?" Doan asked, but Hart only smiled. "All right, be a love and call me if you think of anything else. And I may call on some of your legendary private detectives, though I have a pretty good opinion of one certain police detective. I might even be . . . willing to do a few more divorce cases."

Dollar signs glittered in Hart's eyes. "Doan, my resources are at your disposal."

"Really, darling," Doan insisted to Stan through the jail's waiting room glass, "this is for the best."

"Swell. And how much longer do you think I can save myself for you in here?"

Doan made an unpleasant face. "I'll talk to Luke

115

and see what he can do about getting you a room of your own, all right, angel?"

"They're called cells, light of my life."

"Yes, yes. But this really is the best place for you. No one can accuse you of anything while you're in here."

Stan narrowed his eyes at Doan. "Got a question for you. What if, as long as I'm in here, no one else gets murdered?"

Doan smiled. "I have that all taken care of." He rose. "Have to go acquit you, love. If it helps, I got a message from Binky on my machine, and she's on to something. So just you hold tight. Kiss, kiss."

Binky was on her couch when Doan let himself in. "You know," she said as soon as the door shut, "you're absolutely right."

"Of course I am," Doan said, coming into the living room. "What am I absolutely right about this time?"

"Someone is framing Stan."

"No? Really? Do tell."

"I'll tell you all about it as soon as you make us some coffee."

"Why me? No, never mind, I know. I'm the maid. Fine, I'll bill you for this whole afternoon."

The doorbell rang. "Get that, will you?" she said, lost in thought.

Doan gritted his teeth and started to say something, but he'd already noticed that his retorts were having little or no effect on Binky. "Fine," he said darkly, opening the door to find KC.

"Keep her occupied, would you, so she'll stop making these unreasonable demands on me." KC shut the door behind him.

"Hi," Binky said, sitting up. "Do you have a pen and some paper?"

Doan looked at him and rolled his eyes. "Told you."

"I've been thinking," she announced.

"Good thing," Doan responded. "For a minute, I thought you'd had a stroke, and that as far as you were concerned you were a child back in the family bosom with a hundred servants to do your every bidding."

"I went to that gallery today." She gave the details of her afternoon.

"How hideous," Doan cried. "Let me get you that coffee." There was little in the world that could arouse Doan's sympathy, but when a friend suffered a shock to the sensibilities, he was all comfort and solicitude. "Did she make you look at this stuff, too?" he asked with distaste, holding with his fingertips a flyer she'd brought back from the gallery, announcing a big to-do that night for a big-name East Coast artist.

"No, I got out just in time. Didn't even have to buy anything, thank God. But at least we got a clue. Which I'm going to pass on to Luke, just as soon as I finish this cup of coffee—"

"Ummm . . ." Doan interrupted her. "Maybe you shouldn't do that," he said, allowing the flyer to come closer to his person as he examined it.

"What? Why not?"

"Well, what can he really do with that, after all?" he began to rationalize. "Wouldn't he need a court order to make the gallery owners tell him who bought all the dead man's work? And even if he found out, that might tip the killer off to the fact that the cops were on to him."

Binky regarded Doan suspiciously. "What are you up to, Doan?"

"No good," KC decided.

"You'll see. Just . . . just keep that little tidbit to yourself for a while, okay?"

"Doan . . ." she began to protest.

"Until tomorrow morning," he said, half asking and half declaring.

"Until tomorrow morning," she caved in.

"Good. That's settled. Now, anyone for more coffee?"

Doan was a law-abiding citizen, sort of. That is to say, he abided by laws that made sense to him. Laws against robbery, arson, rape, and such seemed eminently sensible. Laws against murder seemed sensible, too, unless it was someone really awful you were killing, like a robber, arsonist, or rapist, and in that case you should be free to do a little justice. Laws against breaking and entering made sense, too. But he wasn't really planning to break in anywhere, after all, just . . . sort of . . . get in under false pretenses. But it was all to free an innocent man, after all, and he wasn't really going to take anything, just . . . sort of . . . look around.

After leaving Binky's, his plan percolated in his mind. As soon as Binky had reported her failure to extract a name, he'd known that he'd have to get into Le Gallerie on his own to find out who'd purchased Arbuthnott's last works. The only problem had been timing, but the flyer had solved that problem. Once home, he'd called Art.

"Talk to me," Art answered the phone.

"Art, my love, did you by chance get an invitation to a . . ."

"Yes," Art cut him off. "If it is within one hundred miles of here, I got an invitation." Doan heard Art grunt as he hoisted a box full of unopened mail onto his desk. "Where?"

"Le Gallerie."

Art began to shuffle through the box. "I'll find it. What's up?"

"You're taking me there tonight, a party for Claudius Brautwurst."

Art laughed. "You're kidding, right? That's better than John Sex."

"No, that's his real name. And with a name like that, how could he be anything but an artist?"

"Or an accountant. Or a popcorn magnate. Here it is. Ugh!"

"What?"

"Someone spilled coffee all over . . . oops. That's one of Claudius Brautwurst's paintings, printed on the cover of the invitation. Sorry."

"No problem."

"Are you sure we have to go? Can't I send you as my emissary?"

"No, Art. I need you there with me. You've got to point out all the incredibly rich collectors to me, help keep me sane in the midst of all those horrible people and, at a certain time in the evening, cover for me."

"What are you talking about?"

"You're better off not knowing. That way, if I get caught, you can honestly admit you had no idea what I was up to."

"Doan, if my not buying your items anymore has gotten you in some kind of financial trouble, let me know. Please, don't turn to a life of crime. I'd have no one left to amuse me if you went to jail."

"I have no intention of leaving you unamused. I'm just going to find a way to take a peek at their client register and see who bought out the last works of Mortimer Arbuthnott the Third, artist and victim of the SoMa Killer."

Art digested this. "You think someone killed him to make the value of his works go up?"

"It's the first clue we've had, and there's no time to waste. I've got the most adorable little thing waiting for me to get it out of prison, and time's a'wastin'. Pick me up at seven, will you, there's an angel."

• • •

Doan and Art arrived fashionably late at the gallery, which was a warehouse one could conceivably say had been converted, if one counted the addition of track lighting and a deafening sound system as sufficient redecoration, and if one appreciated the ambience of the grease and oil stains on the concrete floor, the lingering particles of some industrial fiber (that got Art sneezing immediately), and several pieces of heavy machinery that had been left by the previous tenants. Ambient house music burbled like aural bubble bath in the background.

Never let anyone tell you that names don't mean anything. Claudius Brautwurst was just what the name implied. Beefy, admittedly, but in a most unappetizing way. His forearms were strong but pudgy, connected by thin elbows to strong, pudgy upper arms, and so on, so as to appear to Doan at first look like a string of sausages twisted into the shape of a man. "You're right," he was telling someone as Doan and Art entered the gallery, "I am rude. And obnoxious. And drunk. You know what else I am? Brilliant. Rich. Hung like a horse." Doan visualized this, based on the look of the rest of him, and decided celibacy had its appeal. "I have rights you don't have, because of that. That's life."

"You owe me a hundred free items," Art hissed at Doan.

"Mr. *Mill!*" a woman shrieked across the room from them, and began to fly toward them. She had

121

the rictus smile and drawn neck tendons of the well-starved. Doan half expected her to take flight, go "awk awk," land on Art's head, and start pecking. "What a *thrill!*"

Art smiled. "Thank you so much for inviting me." Like Doan, a veteran of the cocktail circuit, his skills in such situations were great. "Such a pleasure to see all these new artists."

She began to quiz him in the most unsubtle terms about how much column space she could expect the next day, and Doan took advantage of this moment to steal off on his own. He marked the social architecture of the gathering: The young people in black, obviously the artists being presented along with Brautwurst tonight, were gathered around the nonfunctional machinery in the center, which on closer inspection was revealed to have been gutted and made into a bar. Along the walls, where the paintings were displayed a suitably alienated distance apart, were the guests this show was obviously meant for: silver-haired husbands and their tiny wives. Doan noticed that most of them had in attendance a third person, who he presumed would be their personal curator. He moved closer to one party to hear what sort of wording they used to justify their undoubtedly high salaries to their employers.

"Sure, the Crash of '29 caused the end of Modernism," the man was saying, "as the big buyers were drained of assets in the Crash. The Crash of '87, that's a whole different story. Contemporary artists are seen as an investment now, which they weren't seen as back then. They'll tell you the bottom fell out of the art market in '90; that's not true. It's like an IPO, you just have to get in early. The resale value on a Brautwurst, for instance, well! A year ago, five thousand bucks for a big canvas; now, you could turn that same canvas around for, oh," he whipped a calculator out of his jacket, "say, a hundred seventy five grand."

The wife grabbed the husband's arm. "Get one. Now!"

"Hold on!" the man went on, almost physically holding them back. "Forget Brautwurst. He's old news, you missed the boat. Concentrate on these unknowns. Go to all these shows, buy everything by one particular artist that you can."

"Which one?" the husband asked.

"Doesn't matter. Just get seen at these openings. Hire a press agent to get your picture in the papers. Get a reputation as a collector. You do that, then they'll notice who you're collecting, bam! Prices on the guy go through the roof. You sell half, you donate the other half to museums."

"Just . . . give them away?" the husband asked.

The man put a hand on the husband's shoulder and started walking him away from the old news. "Absolutely. Look, drop by my office tomorrow morning. I'll show you how to use those donations to shave off all the taxes on all the profits you make on all the other stuff."

Good Lord, Doan thought, as he looked with new eyes at the third party in every scene and noticed the number of calculators being whipped out. They haven't brought their curators—they've brought their accountants!

"Crap!" he heard in Art's unmistakable voice.

"But . . ." the hostess was spluttering, as a crowd drew around to hear the famous columnist.

"Garbage. Look at all this!" he shouted, waving a hand around. "All these attractive, healthy, and well-to-do young people, with nothing but time on their hands, and what do they do with these gifts so rare in the world? This! This phony alienation, this fashionable disgust. These aren't criticisms of mass culture, they're not even ironic tributes to it. They're part of it! You're not mocking Michael Jackson or the Jetsons, you're celebrating and affirming them and validating everything cheap in our culture."

His angry eyes swept the crowd. "You have the nerve to dismiss the old masters as irrelevant, while you enshrine *Gilligan's Island*. You have the nerve to dismiss the classics of Western literature, while you bow down before *Charlie's Angels*. *Shame on you!*" he shouted, masking the soft click as the office door shut behind Doan.

On the other side, Doan smiled to himself. Art Mill was feeling better already.

The room was not only devoid of filing cabinets, but of papers. There was a desk made out of a door laid on a pair of wooden horses, but as it was covered in graffiti, it was no longer a door on a pair of wooden horses but rather a work of art. There was a phone on one side, a personal computer on the other. Doan sat down at the desk in a chair that looked like the bastard child of a director's chair raped by a leather-man's sling. He turned on the computer and waited. He was presented with a baffling menu that gave him options for word processing, databases, accounting, and so on. Accounting seemed most likely to hold the information he was looking for. A dizzying array of possible files were presented for his inspection along with an option to copy these files to another disk. Mercifully, there was a box labeled Blank Formatted beside the machine, which he took to mean usable. Files called "SALES1" and "SALES2" made eminent good sense to him, and he copied them from the computer to the floppy disk, and then copied some more files for the hell of it, and kept copying until he was informed that he'd filled his disk. He turned off the computer, tucked the disk inside his purse, and hoped he could sneak out as easily as he'd snuck in.

He was in luck. As he'd assumed, Art was long gone, waiting in the car for him. But Claudius Brautwurst was holding forth eruditely.

"Fuck 'im! Fuck 'im! He wants to fuck with me, I'll punch his fuckin' lights out. Where is he? Where is he?" Cameras appeared from nowhere and began flashing to capture the sight of the great genius being held back from the door by one man while one on the other side tried to wipe the spilled wine off Braut-wurst's shirt. "I'll make him cry. You bet your ass I'll make him cry!"

The pictures in the paper the following day caused a revival of interest in Brautwurst, who had been out of fashion for a month or so, and prices jumped on his works again. The husband and wife who had been talked out of buying any Brautwurst, of course, fired their accountant.

Doan got into the car and slammed the door with a groan. "Is even the most wonderful man in the world worth all this?"

"You find anything?"

"Yes and no. I never knew you were so passionate about art!"

"I'm not. I got Anthony Chamberlain, our art critic, to write something I could memorize. Pretty damning stuff, eh?"

"You bad man. Well, never mind all that for now. Let's eat before I perish."

Hunger made them reckless, and they ended up at a new restaurant on Folsom in the heart of SoMa. The green floor, pink tables, black and white chairs, and loud synthesized music, combined with the standard-issue black and brown paintings on the walls were enough to dissuade Art's appetite, but Doan pulled him on in. "Two, please. Come on, this is nothing after that depression factory," he insisted as they followed the host to their table. "And right now, I don't even care if it's nouvelle, I'm starving. We'll just order six of whatever we want."

Doan thought he had prepared himself for the worst by assuming nouvelle. Upon opening the menu, however, confusion set in.

"What is this?" Art demanded to know. "Birth School Work Death, fourteen ninety-five; Loneliness and Shopping, thirteen ninety-five; Three Minutes to Midnight, twenty-one ninety-five?"

There were no descriptions underneath these titles to indicate what one would be ordering. Doan caught a waiter. "Are you ready to order?"

"Well, no. What's Three Minutes to Midnight?"

"An expression of grief, a feeling of emptiness, of hopelessness."

"That's not terribly appetizing. I'll take Love and Death." He turned to Art. "It's thirty bucks, so maybe there's some food on the plate."

Their meals arrived quickly, to their dismay. Love and Death turned out to be a white plate with a small target propped up on it, a heart painted in the target's center, next to a spent bullet lying on a bed of lettuce. "Could I get Roquefort?" Doan asked. The waiter gave him an affronted look and disappeared, not, presumably, to comply with the request.

Art had ordered Loneliness and Shopping, and discovered himself the lucky possessor of an entire tomato, albeit a tomato studded with pieces of a cut-up charge card. Juice leaked from the punctured

127

tomato onto the sheaf of charge card receipts underneath.

Doan examined this still life for a moment, blinked, then cleared all but the lettuce off his plate with a sweep of his hand. After chopping the lettuce, he picked up Art's tomato and began destudding it. "Get rid of those papers, why don't you?" He quickly and expertly sliced the tomato up over the lettuce, tossed it all together, and pushed half of it onto Art's plate. "Behold. Salad Angst. I'll sell it back to them for fifty bucks."

They ate their semimeals quickly, for fear that someone would see them actually consuming food and throw them out. Afterward, Art leaned forward. "There, that'll hold me for about half an hour. So, what do you think all of Arbuthnott's stuff being sold has to do with the murders?"

"Maybe nothing. After seeing what I saw tonight, it doesn't surprise me that someone would buy up every available piece by some nobody, on the not-so-off chance that tomorrow he'll be somebody. And whoever did buy it probably would have turned it all around in a day for a hundred percent profit, even if Arbuthnott was still alive. Still, it's a lead to check out."

"So when did you become a detective?"

"So it's a lead for the police to check out, then."

Art chuckled. "You sound so serious, Doan."

"You'd be serious if your boyfriend was in jail for murder, too."

"No doubt I would be. But are you sure he's innocent?"

"Oh, yes," Doan said calmly.

"You know, I hate to be the one to tell this to you, but, well, it's always the nice ones who end up being the guilty ones."

"I know. But Stan's innocent. And I never said he was *nice*."

Art shrugged. "If you say so."

"The cops, with the exception of Luke, are trying to pin all the murders on Stan, quite foolishly. One: The murder before last was done by someone who a, knew a lot about electricity, b, had access to a lot of recording and editing equipment, and c, had the money to acquire twenty TVs and twenty VCRs. Stan knows nothing about electricity, recording, or editing. He's a painter. Not only does he not have the money for all that technology, he has no charge cards and, like a real artist, he has bad credit, so he couldn't have rented any of it. And how about transporting it all there? Stan not only doesn't have a car, he doesn't know how to drive. Consequently, we are talking about either a, someone else with all these skills, unlikely, or b, a bunch of people, some of whom were perhaps unwitting accomplices in the whole thing. Like whoever got all the machinery together.

"Two: The murder before that involved putting a body alongside a number of mannequins on a park bench and covering the whole thing with plaster. Once again, money and manpower.

"Three: The first murder was simple enough, I grant you, but the artist in question was picked up and hurled onto that bed of glass they found him impaled on. Stan is, I must say, most attractive in a wiry sort of way, but he's by no means the type who's capable of hoisting bodies about. The killer was, I believe, a, someone who knew both Arbuthnott and Stan, and so learned of Stan's little note, and b, planned to do him in anyway, and used the note as the inspiration for this latest method of murder, sure that it would bring suspicion on Stan. Which is really pretty dumb, when you consider how unqualified he was for the first three murders.

"My theory is that someone's buying up these artists' work, then killing them off to increase the value, which seems fairly silly, since you don't even have to die anymore for your price to go through the roof, though death is still a guarantee that it will. So," he summed up, "the killer is one or more people, who have one or more of the following: wealth, greed, stupidity, impatience, and murderous tendencies. And let's not rule out a side order of vengeance somewhere along the line, mind you."

"My God, I never knew what kind of analytical mind you were hiding. Why the hell didn't you go to college?"

"For what? To qualify for some job where I'd not only have to be there during," he shuddered, "appointed hours every day, but where I'd have to wear men's clothes?"

"Good evening gentlemen," said the man who sat down at their table. "I am the proprietor. I have been tirelessly working for decades to bring art to the masses—"

"*Run!*" Doan shouted, making a break for the door. Art threw a hundred dollar bill on the table and smiled apologetically. "Performance artist—he's rehearsing," he explained, following hot on Doan's heels.

The next day, Doan met Binky outside KC's apartment building. "I am not happy."

"Of course not," she consoled him, having already heard the complete details of his previous evening on the phone that morning. "I'm so sorry, but it has to be this way. Here," she offered him a paper bag. He opened it and examined its contents. His head came back up with a smile.

"Florence Nightingale has nothing on you, angel." As Binky had figured it would, two bottles of White Star and an intimidatingly large pink bakery box had mollified Doan's mortification at having to visit KC on his, as Doan had put it, "own stomping grounds."

"Now come on," she insisted, all business again. He sighed and followed her into the building, clutching his paper bag for consolation.

"Nah yew wach at fer dem buffalo chips, missy," Doan twanged at her outside KC's door.

"Stop that." She rang the bell.

KC opened the door and ushered them in. Much to

Doan's surprise, it seemed to all intents and purposes
to be a perfectly normal apartment. The wood floors
were well polished and overlaid with a mélange of
Southwestern rugs. Doan was disappointed to find
that the walls were not only not adorned with the
presupposed Rockwells and Remingtons, nor with
cheesy beefcake posters tastefully framed, but with
(he shuddered) some of the very artists he had on his
own walls: prints of Dali, Hockney, and Georgia
O'Keeffe. Small gratification was at last to be had in
the bathroom. There, KC at last had a typical gay
picture: a small print of the famous Hippolyte Flan-
drin male nude, curled up in the fetal position on a
rock (a picture most famous now for its use in viatical
settlement advertisements). Alas, there were no little
round sissy soaps in the bathroom to give the game
away, but no pretentiously butch colognes such as
Brut or Stetson, either.

"Hmph," was all he allowed as he made his was
back into the living room, where Binky and KC were
waiting patiently. Binky had tried to restrain Doan
from immediately prowling through every room, but
KC had waved her off. "Let him."

"It'll do. Where's that machine of yours?"

KC led them to his guest room/office, and turned
on his PC. "Do you by any chance remember the
name of the program?" he asked Doan.

"Something delicate and Japanese-sounding. I remember it being a perfectly preposterous thing to
name an unattractive table of numbers."

"Thank God for your easily affronted sensibilities," KC said, for which Doan had no answer, not quite sure if he was being complimented or not. KC typed "Lotus" at the computer's prompt.

"That's it. Here's the disk."

KC tapped keys, information moved on the screen, Doan yawned loudly. KC did not fail to notice. "This might take some time. Why don't you dig into your goodie bag?"

Doan eyed him. "How'd you know what was in here?"

He smiled. "I know you. I know Binky. I know you didn't want to come here. I know what Binky would use to get you here."

"Hmph," Doan repeated, for lack of a better response, and took his bag into the kitchen. Binky followed and shut the door behind them.

"Here," she said. "Eat."

Doan attacked the box. "Oooh, yum. Napoleons. Mmm. So," he said between bites, "what's the deal?"

"KC's going to try and figure out if you got the right files, for starters. Then, if you did, he's going to see if he can't find out who bought Arbuthnott's stuff. Then we're going to call Luke." She glared at him balefully. "As we should have in the first place. And God only knows how I'm going to explain to an officer of the law that the lead I'm giving him was illegally obtained, and thus probably useless."

Doan swallowed hastily. "Don't be silly. It's called inverse police procedure. First, we find out if the info is any use, then, if it is, Luke files the proper papers to get it the legal way, so that it's admissible evidence in court, but while we're waiting for permission, we use it to find the killer, before the killer gets tipped off that we're getting permission to find out who he is. Get it? Mmph, yummy. What else is in that box?"

She handed him a kiwi tart. "I know you said the killer was stupid, but you don't really think he left his name in blood, so to speak?"

"No, but at least now we have the start of a paper trail."

"Doan, what is this? *Police procedure, admissible evidence, paper trail.* Did you go to law school last night or something?"

"Well, yes, so to speak. Here, have a glass of champagne."

She took it, but still stared at him, awaiting an answer.

"All right. I already talked to Luke."

"You did?!" she said, irritated that she hadn't been the first to get the scoop, and relieved that she hadn't been the one to have to tell him and be subjected to a lecture on improper procedure.

"Last night. Woke him up, to make sure he was too groggy to properly give me what for. Besides," Doan drew up with a flush of pride, "he thinks I did the right thing, all things considered." He grinned.

Binky shook her head. "If your powers of charm are no longer limited to wealthy, attractive, gay men, we are all in trouble."

"Charm? Ha! Reason, my dear. Sheer brainpower."
KC interrupted them. "I've got something."

They huddled around the computer. "You see here," KC pointed, "this is the list of represented artists, here's the dates of sales, how much, to who. They sold sixteen Mortimer Arbuthnott canvases in one day, two days before he was killed. For a total of two hundred and fifty thousand dollars."

"Where *did* I hide those crayons?" Binky asked. "I *must* get to work at once."

"And according to this, the purchaser was one Steven Alholm."

"Arrest him!" Doan shouted.

"Not proof," Binky said.

"Well," KC said, leaning back and putting his hands behind his head, eminently pleased with himself, "there's another record in a different part of this spreadsheet for Mr. Alholm." He moved the cursor to the top half of the split screen. "Yesterday, Le Gallerie purchased half of those works back. For three hundred and seventy five thousand dollars." Binky gave a low whistle.

"They must all have the same accountant," Doan muttered.

"What's that?"

"Never mind."

"Anyway, that's the story on him. Except." He paused dramatically.

"Go on," Doan practically shouted.

"Steven Alholm is also listed here," flip, flip, went

the screen, "as the agent for an artist named Stanley
Parks."

"Stan?" Binky and Doan asked in unison.

"Stan," he confirmed.

There was a knock at the door. "Erase it!" Doan
did shout this time. "Hurry!"

"What?"

"That's Luke at the door. I told him to meet us
here. Oh, if he finds out that Stan's connected to the
murderer . . ."

"That doesn't mean anything, Doan."

"Oh, no, not to us. But to the police, who have no
instincts, who don't know Stan, who have only mere
reason to go on, well . . ."

Binky let Luke in. "Good morning, and welcome
to Atkinson, Van de Kamp, and McCandler, Inc.,
Detectives."

"Atkinson? Who's Atkinson?" Doan demanded.
KC raised his hand. "No. Really? I didn't think you
had a last name. Does this mean you'll now tell us
what KC stands for?"

"No. Wait—yes, when you tell me how you got a
name like Doan."

Doan blushed, the first time Binky had ever seen
him do so. "Never mind."

"Come here, look at this," Binky said, leading
Luke to the computer.

"Oh, woe and misery," Doan wailed, consoling
himself with another kiwi tart.

A few minutes later, having been filled in by KC,

Luke assured Doan that it did not, after all, mean woe and misery for Stan. "As a matter of fact," he said, "it helps."

"How?"

"Let's assume this Alholm is or works with the killer. He bought Arbuthnott's works before he died, right? So say he uses that as an excuse to go and see Arbuthnott—I am your patron, etc., etc. Arbuthnott shows him the note he's just received from Stan. Planning to kill him anyway, or knowing he's going to be killed, Alholm decides to frame Stan, throwing all suspicion on him. Now our suspect, Alholm, is tied in to Stan, which shows how easily Alholm could frame him. See?"

Binky sat down. "My head hurts. I just want to go home and read a fashion magazine."

"Go shopping," Doan chimed in.

"Get la—" she stopped short, blushing. Luke smiled his killer smile. Doan fanned himself.

"But, yes, you were right, Doan. It's information worth having. And we'll get it through channels, eventually. Now, does anyone know Alholm?" They all shook their heads. "Know of him?" Negative again. "In that case . . ."

"Stan." Doan said. "Of course. Let's ask Stan."

"Get your coats," Luke said, heading for the door.

FIVE

❧

"ALHOLM? STEVEN ALHOLM? YOU'VE NEVER HEARD OF him?" Stan asked them disbelievingly.

"And why on earth should we have heard of him?" Doan asked.

"He's only a household word in the art world. He was one of the first artists' agents, and he's still the most successful. You see, it used to be that artists would deal directly with galleries. A gallery owner would pick you up and become the sole seller of your works. Alholm changed all that. He became the intermediary between the gallery and the artist, but he wasn't exactly an agent. He would buy your works, probably everything you had, and then he'd sell them to the galleries. It never would have worked back before art prices got so crazy, but an artist's loyalty to a gallery can end pretty fast when someone like Alholm offers to buy everything they've got at once, whereas a gallery sells on consignment."

"So it's like cornering the market, except that it's legal," Luke asked.

"Right. The question with Alholm always was, where did the money come from? See, sometimes he'd buy up some total unknown, but rarely. He's like a shark, always cruising the waters for food. He'll hear of someone who's on the verge of discovery, but who's still undervalued, and he'll pay them a lot more than they're getting at their current gallery."

"And you were one of his . . . discoveries?" Luke asked.

"Well, yes and no. I mean, I was, for a minute. When I first moved into my loft, there were some boxes left behind from this novelty company that had the building before it got converted. They were full of these little, maybe two-inch-high plastic skeletons with moving joints. So I started messing around with them. I made some chairs from paper clips and some hair from stuffed animals, and started making little tableaus. I'd take one skeleton and stand it behind another seated one, and I'd glue its joints into a pose that made it look like it was doing the hair of the other one. There was this one where I made them little papier-mâché sunglasses and put them out on deck chairs made from matchbooks, or sat them at tea with little Barbie teacups, stuff like that."

"What's with you and skeletons, anyway?" Doan asked.

Stan ignored him. "It was just jokey stuff, nothing serious. But I put it in a show and called it All Is Vanity. I sold them all in one night, and saw them in *ArtForum* a month later. Then I heard the company that had moved out of my building was being besieged with pleas from artists across the country for boxes of little skeletons."

"So Steven Alholm heard about this fabulous trend and was immediately on your doorstep."

"For a minute. I made a bunch more skeleton figures, even though I didn't feel too good about it. The first ones were a joke, and they were fun. This was like . . . well, that building I live in used to be a factory, and it started to feel like it was a factory again. I made a lot of money real fast off those, but when he saw the stuff I normally do, my paintings, that was it. Not trendy enough. I didn't have an agent anymore."

Luke leaned back and absorbed this. This accounted well enough for Alholm's name being associated with Stan's in Le Gallerie's books. But it didn't cast any suspicion on Alholm. The purchase of all of Arbuthnott's works just before the murder now looked less like a motive, as it could be just another move in an Alholm sales strategy, a strategy that would capitalize on death but did not necessarily involve murder.

"Well," Doan said. "Well, well, well." He got up and stretched, adjusting the collar of the peach blouse that went so well with the black Chanel suit that said, "I mean business." He felt for all the world like a young lawyer on his first big case. "Very interesting. Lots to work with here."

Stan looked at him. "Are you kidding? There's zilch, that's nothing that's gonna get me off."

"No," Doan agreed. "But now we have another suspect. Someone who worked with the last dead man, and had to have at least known the others. Someone who, from this history we've gotten today, is perfectly awful. Thank God you're a gossip hound." Stan meant to protest, but Doan went on. "He's someone who knows Stan and has no use for him when he discovers that this fit that sparked these perverse little objects was only temporary." He turned to Luke. "Am I brilliant, or what?"

Luke smiled. By all the rules in the book, Doan had no business in the interrogation room. However, he'd been quick to point out to Captain Fisher that she owed him one for putting Flaharity on the case. Doan's self-deputization as an investigator had gone to his head, admittedly. The minute he heard that Captain Fisher had been cajoled into not noticing that he'd been allowed into the interrogation room, he'd insisted on stopping at home to change, stopping at Macy's to purchase a briefcase and a Filofax, and stopping at a stationer's for legal pads and various bric-a-brac with which to fill said new briefcase.

"A veritable Sherlock Holmes," Luke agreed, shutting his notebook. "So is that the whole story on Alholm?"

"Everything I know. And if there's anything else,

it's got to be hidden pretty deep to have stayed off the grapevine this long."

"Okay, thanks. We'll keep you filled in. Come on, Doan."

"Umm . . ."

"Uh-oh." Luke had already learned the meaning of this sound when it came from Doan.

Doan pulled him to a corner of the room. "Did your boss say anything, by any chance, about what it takes to get a . . ." he fell to a whisper, ". . . conjugal visit?"

"Forget it."

Doan sighed and shrugged. "Worth a shot."

Later that day, Doan got a call at home from Binky. "I got a message on my machine from your friend."

"One has so many."

"Eleanor Ambermere. Why don't you get an answering machine?"

"I'm not sure. Probably for the same reason I don't have a goatee, or a car, or wear men's clothes. Just out of spite, because everyone else in the world does. Besides, why should I get a machine when people I really want to talk to have *your* number and can leave me a message on yours?"

"What! I should be charging you for services rendered!"

"Calm down. The circulation's limited. Eleanor has your number, Stan will have it as soon as we get his luscious self out of jail, and Luke has it, of course. Doesn't he?" he asked slyly.

"Yes," she answered primly. "He does. Do you want your message?" she asked, changing the subject.

Doan sighed, temporarily defeated. "Yes."

"Just that she hadn't heard from you since you got back, aside from your message that all was well. What were those papers, anyway?"

"Oh, that!" Doan cried. If any reader has forgotten about the papers of Eleanor Ambermere, they cannot be blamed, for in all the excitement of love and danger the last few days, Doan himself had also completely forgotten. "Aside from being the dirt on Charles Ambermere, I don't exactly know. Eleanor said it was best that I didn't. Well, I'll give her a buzz."

"A buzz? How professional you sound."

"I am a professional. I work for the Police Department, you know."

"No, you don't, you just . . . wait a minute. Doan, you don't just get to see Stan with this bit, am I right?"

"What?" Doan asked innocently.

"You're getting another paycheck!" she accused. "How many is that now? Four?"

"Not exactly. Even I can't get around civil service tests and academy training and all that silliness involved in actually *working* for the Police Department. But, you know, there are ways of getting reimbursed for one's expenses related to criminal investigations . . ."

"Not another word, ever, about my trust fund."

"Of course not, dear," he said in surprised and gentle tones. "I understand completely how hard it is to be well off and unemployed. Ta!"

But before she could splutter her rage and denial, the line was dead in her hands.

She slammed it down and it rang again immediately. "How dare you?" she accused.

"My father warned me that women would always be angry with me for no reason a man could see," Luke said.

"Oh, I'm sorry. I thought it was Doan."

"Well, that explains that. Listen, what are you doing tonight?"

"Nothing," she said. "Why?"

"Oh, just thought I'd drop by. See how you were."

For reasons unknown to her, she panicked. "Well, okay, if you're sure you aren't too busy."

"Too busy to see you? In the long run, what could be more important that seeing you? Doan's on the SoMa Killer case now, so the killer's as good as caught."

She laughed nervously. "Sure." She tried one last evasive tactic. "I don't have anything to eat."

"I'll pick up Chinese."

"Or drink."

There was a pause. "If you don't want to, just let me know."

"Oh, no, it's not that I don't want to, really . . ." She groped for words.

"No, you're right," he said calmly. "It was just a passing thing, the pressure and all. I'm much too busy to come over. Well, see you around."

"Wait!"

He waited.

"I'm sorry. I'm just really nervous right now. I don't usually . . ." She groped for a way to say that she didn't usually see the men she slept with twice without sounding like someone awful. Doan's voice in her head, drawling that God forbid any old fling know where she lived and be able to find her, taunted her. It's true, it's true, she wailed, I'm an emotional virgin. "Would you believe I don't know anything about dating?"

She could hear him relax. "Yeah. I would." He lowered his voice to a silky growl that drove her straight out of her skin. "But I also know you're a very fast learner."

"Well . . ."

"Why don't you come over to my place?" She realized he was offering her, if not neutral territory, at least a place she could leave if she so wished. He was giving her so much room, more than she had the nerve to ask for! Dammit, he was making it impossible not to love him. "I'll get us that Chinese."

"Okay," she heard herself say with a mixture of relief and trepidation. "I'll see you in an hour."

She hung up and looked out the window. "It's just

a date," she said. "I spent three nights in bed with him, and thought nothing of it. So why does sitting across a table from him terrify me?"

Frannie answered the phone. "Van Owens."

"At last," Doan sighed. "When did you stop saying Ambermere?"

"Yesterday. Here she is."

Eleanor came on the phone. "And a fine thank you I get, for all that money I gave you. How much is left?"

"Not a cent."

"I knew it. Have a good time in Bermuda?"

"Well . . . yes and no." He filled her in.

"Cheer up. The one that got away always looks better than the one you get."

"Speaking of getting away, I take the change in phone announcement means that the Bulbous One is officially gone?"

"He cleaned out his closet yesterday. Actually, Frannie cleaned it out for him. Onto the sidewalk. He got to it just before the Salvation Army did."

"Hoorah!"

"Yeah. Except . . ."

"What?"

"Can you come over?"

"Can you send that big black car?"

"Yes."

"Yes."

• • •

147

An hour later, Doan was ensconced in a leather wingback chair in Charles's . . . what used to be Charles's study. A fire crackled, warming the brandy snifters in front of it. Eleanor was chugging on a cigar.

"Havana," she shouted, waving it about. "Best in the world, available only to those with access to diplomatic pouches out of Cuba. Bought with my money, kept in humidors with my money, smoked by people who were practically given my money. Considering how much of my money ended up having something to do with these goddamn cigars, I think I'd smoke 'em even if I didn't like 'em."

"Last time I was here," he said, irritably waving the smoke away, "it was just cigarettes. What's next?"

"Pot," she said firmly, as if she'd just decided.

"Eleanor!"

"Just kidding."

"So what did you want to see me about?"

"Just to celebrate the end of Charles."

"Come on."

"I'm just thinking . . . he really didn't care when I told him about the papers. I know him inside out. As long as I didn't turn them over to anyone, he was happy. Oh, he made a fuss, all right, but he's not an actor. If he was, at least one of his disastrous deals might have come through for him. This means he's got money coming in from somewhere else."

"Another woman." Doan thought of the hateful

little creature at the police station Binky had told him about. "I think it's disgusting, but there really are women out there who think you've wronged him. With your 'antics,' is how they put it."

"Antics?" Her voice slurred. "I saved my country. Those damn collaborators!" She blinked, coming back to herself, then smiled. "You know, that's the first time I've lost it since the last time you were here."

Doan impulsively got up and went around the desk to hug her. "Oh, honey, you're so brave I could scream. You've triumphed over illness, depression, and Charles Ambermere. I believe I shall speak of you to perfect strangers all day today, that I may kill the first little mouse who bad-mouths you."

"You really think it's another woman?"

"That depends."

"On what."

"On what you want to hear. If you want to believe that there's a woman out there who would have that lump of sludge, be my guest. Or, do you want to believe that one of his shady little enterprises may not only have nothing to do with your money, but may be successful?"

She sighed. "It's gotta be that. No woman would want a man that ugly, that mean, and that dumb."

"Now, come on. Tell me. What's he been up to?"

"I'd really rather you didn't know."

"Eleanor. The real purpose of not turning this documentation of yours over to the police was to make him really worry and suffer, the way he wouldn't if you only left him penniless. Now, obviously, he isn't worrying and he isn't suffering. This is against the laws of nature. And I am going to help you make him suffer. Now tell me, what's he involved in?"

She relit the cigar, took a swig of her brandy, and looked out the window.

"Art. That tasteless bastard's screwing around in art. Can you believe that?"

Binky could hear the phone ringing from the top of the stairs. Cursing her own spite, which had made her leave the answering machine off, she ran down the hall, fumbled with her keys, threw the door open, and lunged at the phone. It must be Luke, she'd been telling herself during this great athletic effort, calling to make sure I got home all right. Then, as she was about to pick it up, she remembered that she'd stolen out of the house at dawn, before he'd woken up. He was calling, she was now sure, to ask her why she'd done that. With trepidation, she picked it up.

"Hello?"

There was no voice on the other end.

"Oh, I'm sorry. But I've never . . ." she flushed. "I rarely spend the whole night with a man. I know that must make you think I'm awful, but . . ." she stopped. In the background she could hear a cheerful humming, and the sound of rattling pans, clanking dishes, and running water.

"Hello?" No answer. *"Hey!"* she shouted.

The clanking stopped. *"Hey!"* she screamed.

The water stopped. There was a rustle as the phone was picked up.

"At last," Doan said, "you're home."

"What?" she asked disbelievingly. "What were you doing in the kitchen?"

"Well, I tried to buzz you again last night. No answer, not even the machine. And I had the most desperately important news. So I thought, when you eventually did get home, I'd know the minute you walked in the door."

"Doan. Are you trying to tell me . . . that you let my phone ring . . . for twelve hours?"

"Uh-huh!" he said cheerfully. "Are you ready for this?"

"No."

"Give me Luke's number, so I can call him and have him issue a warrant for the arrest of the SoMa Killer."

"Who?"

"Charles Ambermere."

Doan got into Luke's car and shut the door. "Did you bring the warrant?"

"No, Doan, I didn't. I need to see the proof to get the warrant."

"Well, then, we'll have to stop at Eleanor's before we go arrest Charles."

"If we can arrest Charles."

"Oh, yes, we can, indeed." Doan filled him in on

151

the tactics Eleanor had used for a quick, clean, and cheap divorce.

"Any documentation of crime she had, she should have turned over to the police in the first place."

"That's neither here nor there, now. The point is, I just found out a few interesting things. First, Charles is half owner in Steve Alholm's business. Second, they've been juggling the books in a manner that would befuddle the entire staff of Price Waterhouse. And last, their gallery has been selling works under the table by certain artists that aren't listed in any catalog of their works. All of these artists, by the way, are dead."

Luke stopped the car. "Which ones?"

"Guess."

"All four?"

"All four. Eleanor, alas, never reads the paper, since irritating news is prone to put her back into her other world. If she'd known even one of them was dead, she would've turned those papers over a long time ago. So, in addition to all that fraud, they kill these guys, take their finished works away, and sell them secretly. Oh my God, if . . ."

"What?"

"She told Charles about her proof, but he didn't care, because she said she wasn't going to use it. But what if he told Alholm about it?"

"You don't know?" He started the car, put the siren on the dash, and tore out.

"No. She didn't say." They were both thinking the

same thing. Charles might be just a crook, but that meant that Alholm . . .

They pulled up at Eleanor's house with a screech.

"The front door's open," Doan whispered in horror.

Luke pulled out his gun. "Stay behind me."

They crept up toward the house, keeping low. Luke turned the corner, pointing the gun at whoever might be in the hall. "Come on."

Inside, the house was quiet. They went from room to room on the first floor. No one. Nothing.

At the top of the stairs, they heard a muffled groan. "Frannie," Doan said.

They found a groggy Frannie bound and gagged, one eye turning black. Doan tore off the gag while Luke cased the rest of the floor.

"Eleanor?" Doan asked.

"Charles," she answered, and passed out again.

When someone accused Charles Ambermere of being a mean bastard, a manipulator, and a user, he was truly hurt, despite the fact that he'd never worked an honest day in his life, that everything he had he'd taken from Eleanor Van Owens, and that he had casually bungled everything he'd ever attempted— that is, with the exception of his latest endeavor, which was doing quite well. At long last, he thought, he had found the proper outlet for his moneymaking genius. Vindicated at last! The fact that he'd had to resort to murder, robbery, and fraud to finally become a success did not cross his mind.

He had expensively cut and styled white hair, a bulbous nose, an even more bulbous stomach, and an expression on his red face of perpetual surprise. When he married Eleanor, he had actually been dashing, in that too slender and dangerous way, and it was his looks that had made the Van Owens clan suspicious from the start. Men as handsome as that did not court frail girls like Eleanor for any reason other than money. But Eleanor had been captivated by the charm and good spirits of the man who looked to her so much like Errol Flynn, and since she was over twenty-one when they'd met, and in possession of her full inheritance, there was little the family could do to stop the marriage.

The rest, you already know. That Eleanor had not only lived this long, but even had some money left after Charles had control over it for years, was nothing short of miraculous in itself. In his kindest moments, Charles had taken Eleanor for granted, the goose who laid the golden eggs he kept dropping and breaking. When she had begun careening down the hills of San Francisco, however, he stopped taking her for granted and started taking her to psychiatrists. Not to help her, mind you, but to get her declared senile, at which he had been successful. Deprived of love, money, freedom, everything but the company of Frannie and Doan, it was inevitable that sickly Eleanor become a total invalid.

But when she'd walked into that kitchen, made herself a sandwich, and started yelling . . . the way a rat knows the instant the ship springs a leak, he'd known the end was near. That same day, he'd read in the paper that some stupid painting of some stupid flowers had been sold to some stupid person for fifty-something million dollars. There was even a picture of it reproduced full-color in *USA Today*, his favorite newspaper. He'd stared at that picture while the household outside his study erupted in chaos. Even the arrival of the stupid faggot in the stupid dress had failed to jar him from his reverie. He took a few markers out of his desk, a piece of fresh paper, and idly copied the picture in a few minutes. Then he brooded some more. What he saw in that picture was not a work of art. What he saw in his own surprisingly good copy was not a glimmer of talent in his otherwise uncultured soul. What Charles Ambermere saw was a lot of money and an easy way to make it.

At the same time, Steve Alholm had begun making even more money by beginning a newsletter for the art set that listed in blatant Dow Jones-like tables the current prices that works had gone for in the last week, and prices on works being offered currently. When Charles got a load of the first issue, he immediately made an appointment with Alholm.

"You've got it all wrong," he said. "You could be rich."

Steve Alholm had blazing red hair, glitteringly cold blue eyes, and thin, cruel lips, which he allowed to

155

turn up in bitter amusement at Charles's gall. "Really? I seem to be doing pretty well."

Charles had taken one look at Alholm and known he was a kindred spirit. There would be no need to beat around the bush. "First, stop representing artists. Open your own gallery. Second, hire the most aggressive salesmen you can find."

"Most people with any knowledge and appreciation of art would be appalled at the notion of being aggressive salesmen."

Charles smiled. "Some companies need knowledgeable salesmen. Others only need good salesmen who can be taught the buzzwords."

Alholm smiled. "Go on."

"I'll finance the gallery. You provide the merchandise."

"And your cut?"

"Fifty percent of the profit."

Alholm leaned back in his chair. "That's not a very good business deal. I open a gallery, do extra work, and so I make a few extra thousand off each deal. So what, if I've got to give it to you?"

"You'll have to adjust the prices accordingly in each direction."

"Forget it. My artists are accustomed to quick return on their works, on an escalating scale. No way I'm gonna get them to take less."

"Lie."

"Pardon?"

"Sell something for ten grand. Tell your artist it

went for seven five. Give him his cut of that, take your proper cut, give me my proper cut. Then we divide the other two point five in half."

"And when he reads in my newsletter that it went for ten?"

"Tell him you listed the sale price higher than it went for to increase the value of that and future works. Tell him it means you can sell the next one for ten."

"And then sell it for twelve five. Lie to the artists. Lie to the buyers. Lie to the newsletter readers."

"Exactly."

Then they began to laugh. "But listen: Better than owning a gallery . . ."

Fate could not have thrown two more amoral souls together in any more harmonious convergence. They made more money than either of them dreamed possible. Soon they were selling works for twice what they told the artist they were selling for, and a day that made them less than ten thousand dollars each was a slow one indeed.

Alholm hadn't meant to kill Terence Yellen. But Terence had found out that Alholm really had been selling his works for the price listed in the newsletter, and was demanding his share of the money. The argument in Yellen's studio had become heated, Yellen had slapped Alholm, Alholm had punched Yellen and sent him flying onto one of his glass-shard canvases. He had not been unmoved by the sight of the dead man, the man he had just killed. Actually, he had enjoyed it.

Charles was horrified when Alholm told him that evening. Their game had moved into a whole new level, one he had not been prepared for. But he had been exposed to Alholm for too long, for even as he recoiled from the picture of the dead man that Alholm had so graphically presented, a part of him was calculating. One possibility followed another, falling neatly into place.

They went back to Yellen's studio and appropriated the finished works. No one knew of their existence but the two of them and the dead man; they were able to sell these last works for outrageous prices to buyers who asked no questions regarding the legality of the deal.

Charles picked the next victim, thrilling with the power he held over these men, the power to play God and choose who would live and who would die. He chose Hartley, the sculptor of plaster people, because he'd made fun of Charles's nose one day in the gallery. He told Alholm to begin reserving Hartley's incoming works. When they had a sufficient number of them, Alholm killed him.

Charles must be given credit, in his own way. For he was a genius now, albeit an evil one. The first death had given him the idea for combining the artist and the work at the scene of the crime, to make it look like a series of murders conducted by a sensibility driven mad by modern art. The joke made Alholm fall out of his chair laughing. The withheld works went the way of those of the first dead man, for a fortune, of course.

They'd thoroughly enjoyed killing Mark Pillson, the performance artist. As a performance artist, there wasn't a lot of money to be made off him, but Alholm had made the one mistake of his career several years earlier when he'd signed Pillson to a five-year contract as his exclusive agent, back when the NEA Four were getting a lot of attention. His success, however, was not as immediate as Alholm had hoped. Pillson had been whining about Alholm's not putting enough energy into promoting him, and he had become a bother. They'd had a good time constructing the elaborate setup of televisions, VCRs, and generators, especially since money had been no object, and there was no shortage of street people who'd hoist things about, no questions asked, for the right amount of money.

Alholm had killed Mortimer Arbuthnott not for amusement but out of necessity, as he saw it. Arbuthnott had also discovered Alholm's pricing scheme, but feared Alholm's power in the art world. So he had withheld work from Alholm for months, claiming he was blocked. When he had sufficient stock, he sold them to Le Gallerie. When Alholm had gone there for a party being held to celebrate a show by an artist he wanted to make his own, he'd seen Arbuthnott's pictures and come close to apoplexy. He'd purchased them all on the spot.

He'd gone to Arbuthnott's, pretending to be unaware of his duplicity. Arbuthnott had shown him the note from Stan, and Alholm promptly killed him and easily arranged things to implicate Stan. He thought Stan would be considered a likely candidate to go around killing artists, working as he did slowly but surely while Arbuthnott and his ilk made their fortunes sometimes literally overnight.

With four dead, a fortune made, and a murderer under arrest, Alholm decided that this scheme, which he thought of as his own particular work of art, was over. He looked back upon it with enormous satisfaction, and was eager to sit down with Charles and hash out a new one.

And then Charles had lightly passed on the news that not only had he kept a paper record of every one of their transactions, from the largest sale to a secret buyer to the purchase of the TVs and VCRs for Pillson's death, but that his goddamned no longer senile wife had gotten hold of them. "But not to worry," Charles had said, "because she was just using them to make sure I didn't try to get any money out of her in the divorce, and one thing is sure now, I don't need her—"

Alholm punched him then. Then helped him back up. "Now, Charles, partner, old friend, no hard feelings, all right? Let's sit down over here, have a cigar, and figure out how we're going to kill your goddamn wife."

In a more tolerant world, wherein sexuality would be irrelevant, Doan would have been a general. If there was one thing he was capable of, it was marshaling resources. While the city had its own command center for dealing with Eleanor's kidnapping, Doan was not content to sit idle and wait for them to figure it out. As a consequence, his own apartment was now a command center for a very different set of forces.

There were probably no lesser number of maps with pins, jangling telephones, and people running in and out at the latter location than there were at the former. The difference was that at Doan's, the maps were store-bought MUNI Transit maps, the phones were cellular, and the people consisted of our cast and various sources of information, the variety of which never ceased to amaze Luke.

Doan's command center had been set up the same afternoon as Eleanor's disappearance. Doan's immediate suggestion of his own apartment had thrown Binky's mind off the case momentarily. After all, she had been friends with Doan for six months now and still hadn't seen his apartment. She voiced her objections to this plan based on her certainty that someone as irresponsible as Doan must have an awfully small apartment, though she didn't put it quite like that. Luke assured her that there was no problem there, with a bit of a smile she didn't like.

She unraveled the mystery of that smile when she arrived at the apartment that afternoon, bringing office supplies. The address on Polk had made her wince. No doubt poor Doan, for all his multitudinous little incomes, had to rent a rat trap above one of those porno parlors, and that was why he spent so much time at her place. She resolved to be extra nice to him today and not say anything mean about his enforced squalor.

Polk, however, is a very long street. Much to her surprise, she realized her cab was skirting between Russian Hill and Pacific Heights. Rich people in San Francisco are pathological about their heights; they all live in Pacific Heights or Laurel Heights or Presidio Heights. The very presence of a speed bump outside one's door is excuse enough to proclaim one's neighborhood Something Heights. (Rich people love to live on heights not only so they can look down on the masses, but because they've found that homeless people are not inclined to walk up steep hills, probably because they don't have the energy.)

When the cab stopped before one of the most handsome prewar buildings she'd seen on either coast, she checked the address above the door twice against her scrap of paper. Sure enough, there next to a buzzer, was the name McCandler. Sure enough, Doan's voice answered the apartment phone, "First Precinct."

"I hate you."

"I'll explain later," he said, hanging up and buzzing her in.

Upstairs, the great oak door swung open. The

exquisite wood floor was covered with Oriental rugs, which were in turn covered with papers and people. The leather sofa in the living room was monopolized by more people quarreling over contradictory notes. The kitchen held three Braun coffeemakers going at full steam, emptied as fast as they were being filled by a sweet-faced girl with a tattooed, shaved head.

"Hi," she said. "I'm Soheila. I'm from Death's Head Temporary Services. Here, let me take that stuff."

"Pleased to meet you. Have you seen Doan?"

"In the bedroom. Coffee?"

"Yes, please."

"Jamaican Blue Mountain or Kona?"

"Whatever's ready now, please."

She took her cup back to the bedroom and found Doan on the bed with Luke, poring over a list.

"And how are we all doing this afternoon?" she asked icily.

"Oh, hello," Doan said without looking up at her. "Why don't you give that stuff to Soheila and get some coffee?"

"Already done."

"Well," Doan said to Luke, "then that leaves the galleries Alholm dealt with, the artists' lofts to which he had keys, Charles's warehouse, and his cabin up in the woods."

"I'll dispatch the men. Hi, Binky." He gave her a quick kiss on his way out. "Gotta go."

"Now then," she demanded, "how about you fill me in?"

Doan gathered his papers together. "Sure."

"Death's Head Temporary Service?"

"Uh-huh. Some groovy kids who can type and file, and couldn't live on bicycle messenger wages. 'Service with a Snarl,' they promise. They all go to Le Club; they're my biggest fans. Here I am at last with a position, however temporary, of responsibility. How could I resist helping them out?"

"And the maps?"

"All the places in the city where Charles and Alholm could be hiding Eleanor, that's one color pin. Then we substitute another color pin for each of those when we've looked there. That's what Luke's off to do now. The avenues of escape we've sealed off, another color pin. It's so exciting!"

"You're not taking this very seriously."

Doan sobered. "This is terrible, and I know it. Eleanor is old and frail and she's in the hands of psychotics. I also know that if she lives, she's going to want to make an adventure of this, and if she dies, she's going to want her last thought of me to be that I'm doing something like this. I'm doing everything I can, and I have a miraculous constitutional makeup that does not allow me to get depressed. Consequently, it's behavior as usual."

She blushed. "Sorry."

"No problem."

"Anything I can do?"

"You can help Soheila answer the phones. Look, I've got to go follow a lead now, I'll see you later."

"Hey! Wait!"

"What?"

"Explain this apartment."

"Oh, this," dismissing it with a wave. "A gift from a man who has forgotten me completely by now. It's only a payable to his accountant. And I just furnished it over the years with little gifts."

"Roche-Bobois leather sofas are not little gifts."

"There are men in this world, my dear, who quite literally make enough money in the blink of an eye to pay for such trifles. I simply must go."

"Wait again. I nearly forgot." She pulled out a check and handed it to him with a smile. "Your maid's pay."

Doan returned her smile. "Thanks, love. Rescued from the edge of poverty again."

KC was appointed the bringer of good news to Stan, Doan being too busy to even stop and celebrate his beloved's release.

"Free!" Stan shouted on the steps of the jail, laughing and throwing his head back, the wind blowing his hair about as he let the sun dance on his face. KC felt a pang. It was small wonder that forceful Doan had fallen for such an elemental being. He himself could never attract anyone like Doan. He stopped short. Why would someone like himself, eminently sane and responsible, want to attract anyone like Doan anyway?

"How's Doan?" Stan asked.

"He's currently running the San Francisco Police Department," KC said, not without a bitterness that Stan failed to catch.

"That's my Doan! I tell you, if I hadn't met him, and all this had happened, I'd still be in prison. You can bet on it."

"Anyway, what do you want to do, now that you're free? Hey, let's go get a beer, okay?"

"Yeah, sure. I just want to be home early, so I can call Doan and tell him you got me home safe and sound."

"Yeah. Sure."

"Hey, are you okay?"

"Yeah! Yeah, I'm okay."

"You sure? You're acting kinda weird."

"You know, *Cosmo* tells girls they're not supposed to abandon their friends just because a man comes along. The same ought to apply to men, don't you think? Besides, Doan didn't exactly do all this single-handedly. Some other people helped."

Stan put his arm around KC. "Oh, hey, I'm sorry. I really appreciate everything you've done, all of you. And I'm not trying to ditch you or anything, it's just that, well . . ." He lowered his voice. "I've been in *jail*, you know, for a week."

KC lowered his head, feeling foolish. "Hell. I'm so stupid. Totally inconsiderate. After what you've been through."

"I mean," he whispered, even though there was no one around, "you can't do anything by yourself, you know? 'Cause there's always someone around. For a week, you know what I'm sayin'? So I've got other reasons for *really needing* to see Doan. See?"

KC laughed, as Stan had intended him to. "I do see. But Doan is out right now, so we might as well get a beer and see if we can't take your mind off your . . . pressing problem for a couple of hours. Okay?"

"Okay. Hey," he said, punching KC lightly on the arm, "you're a pal. Let's go."

Doan was wearing a dark blue Dior suit and a white satin blouse, with a liberal dousing of Joy. He was going out to the State Streets, an assemblage of warehouses as far as the eye can see, an area too depressingly reminiscent of his childhood hometown for him to confront it without being swathed in the armor of complete and total glamour.

By one of those fortuitous miracles of which writers are so fond, the empty warehouse next to Charles and Alholm's was occupied by a group of Doan's friends, who had a band (Caring Dad Spanks and Cuddles, a name taken from a personals ad in one of the local gay newspapers) and lived there because a, it was free, as the owner didn't exactly know anyone was living there, and b, they could play as loud as they wanted.

Doan knocked on the little person door that was part of the big truck door. A disheveled character opened it some minutes later. "Oh, hi, Doan. Come on in. Jack's not here."

"Hello, Tim. I'll wait," Doan said.

The warehouse had plenty of skylights, a fact that was more distressing than cheering to the occupants, who were inclined to react to dawn by getting into rather than out of bed. Thus, they had cleverly rigged blackout blinds that could be opened and closed by means of a handle, which Doan now used to open them. Tim groaned loudly. "Do you have to?"

"Yes. Look, dear, I need your help." He filled Tim in on the essential details. "So I need to know if anyone's heard anything unusual from next door."

"Umm, no. Not me, I've been asleep all day. But Jack's been in and out today. If you want to wait for him."

Doan sighed. Seeing an old flame would not exactly be the perfect ending to this most imperfect day. How trying police work was! "Okay, I'll wait."

He didn't wait long. A tall, lanky redhead came in and stopped short at the sight of Doan, perched on a crate in the center of the room. "Hello, Jack."

"You never call," he accused.

Doan sighed. "What can I say? We're just not . . . right for each other."

"You've been seeing Stan Parks."

"Oh, is it all over the place?"

"And now it turns out he's a murderer. See where leaving me gets you?" he ended with a slight smile, indicating that he knew Doan was right.

"In all kinds of trouble, I have to admit. But, look . . ." and he went through it all again for Jack. "Have you seen anything at all?"

Jack thought a moment. "Yeah. Usually there's a truck comes there in the morning and again in the late afternoon." He thought for a second. "But I haven't heard any today. Or yesterday either."

Doan got up—jumped up was more like it—with a chill. Eleanor and the killers could be in the very next building this very second. "A phone, love. Do you have a phone?"

"Sorry. You've got to go to the corner for that."

"They could see me."

"I'll go. Who do you want me to call?"

"My place. The number's—"

"I remember," he said, repeating that wry smile and causing Doan to melt.

"Oh, Jack. If only you didn't prize living in poverty and filth, we could have been so happy."

"If only you understood how I prize independence and time for creative endeavors. I'll go make that call. What should I say?"

"Ask for Luke Faraglione, and tell him to bring six squad cars, sirens off, and a warrant to the back door of the warehouse."

Jack blinked. "You have gotten respectable. Okay, on my way."

It was after dark when Doan met Luke and his men behind the warehouse. "Do you have the key?" Doan asked.

Luke went to confer with his sergeant. "The key."

The sergeant flushed and looked at the ground. "Sir, you're not going to like this."

"What."

"The designated officer failed to procure the key, sir."

"And who is the designated officer, so that I may kick his ass from here to kingdom come?"

"Sergeant Flaharity, sir."

"Flaharity!" he shouted, before remembering that this was to be a silent entry. "Where is he?"

"Um, we don't know. That is, he was supposed to stop at that gallery and pick it up, then come here. He failed to show, sir."

"Sergeant, write this up. Let's see if we can't get Flaharity fired at last."

"Yes, sir."

He returned to Doan and filled him in. "So much for that, huh? Well, we've got the warrant, so we can break the door down, I suppose."

"Hold on." Doan disappeared for a moment and came back with Jack in tow. "If you don't mind something that's probably not quite regulation . . ."

"Go for it."

"Would you do the honors?" Doan asked Jack, who set to picking the lock.

"Would you believe," Doan whispered to Luke, "that this criminal genius, this overgrown urchin, was once the love of my life?"

"You do get around," Luke understated tactfully.

"Okay," Jack said, stepping back.

"You stay outside," Luke ordered Doan, drawing his revolver.

"No problem. Gunfire and I are not good friends."

So Luke led his men into the building. The completely dark building, it turned out. There were either no skylights, or they had been blacked out so well that there might as well not be. The door had opened silently, so the element of surprise was still with them. A light burned in the office at the other end of the building. Luke waved his hand and his men fanned out. There was a creak from the office that froze them all in their tracks. Then the front door slammed, and they began to run.

"Police!" Luke shouted when he got to the office. No response. He whipped around, kicked the door open hard enough to make sure it hit the wall so that he could be sure no one was hiding behind it, then he jumped into the empty room. There was a roar from outside. He ran out the front door onto the street. "Vive la Republique!" a harsh voice shouted from the window of a van just before it turned the corner out of sight. He ran back inside and through the building, herding his men ahead of him. "Dark blue Ford van, late '70's, California plates. Get it!"

"Are you sure it was them?" Doan asked, getting into the car with Luke.

"A hoarse old woman shouting 'Vive la Republique' seemed like the Eleanor you described."

"Oh, God, that means she's slipping again. And the

171

one where she's the French Resistance fighter is the worst one."

"Don't say anything," Luke whispered to Doan, "but someone must have tipped them off. Someone inside the PD."

"Uh-oh."

"Don't worry, Doan. We've practically got them now."

This, unfortunately, was not the case. The moment the van had disappeared around the corner, out of Luke's view, Charles stopped. Alholm jumped out of the back, grabbed at the bottom of the back door, and started pulling. The dark blue paint came off in great sheets, revealing a white van with an extermination company name printed on the side, one of a dozen cars on the freeway on-ramp by the time the squad cars were pulling out.

Neither Charles nor Alholm was worried. The warehouse had been meant to be a refuge only for the day, as it was an obvious place for the police to search. The plan they had formulated the day before under duress was still working smoothly—with one exception.

There was only one reason Eleanor was still alive, and that was the existence of the master set of papers. Their henchman had been adroit in following Doan around the world, undoing Eleanor's precautions. But there was one set left, and only Eleanor knew where that was.

Their problem was, the shock of the kidnapping had sent Eleanor back into her senile dementia. By the time they hit the highway, it was eight hours and counting since she'd slipped back. No amount of cajoling, threatening, or even physical violence (which they were still not ruling out) could extract the location of a set of papers from a woman who was refusing to tell the Nazi swine the number of Resistance fighters and their deployment, a woman who, in short, didn't even know the papers existed. They could only guess that they were in the city somewhere, and so found it advisable not to leave it, despite the scope of the manhunt for them. They were not concerned. There were other, better places to hide than the one they'd just vacated.

"You will never crush us, pigs!" Eleanor shouted from the back of the van.

"Can't you gag her?" Alholm asked.

"No way. We need to know the very instant she comes back."

"How will you know?"

"She's always disoriented, asks where she is. Asks for Frannie, then for that faggot." He smiled and looked at Eleanor in the rearview mirror. "Hear that? Faggot. Cocksucker. He's looking very hard for you, Eleanor. But he won't find you. I've got you, Eleanor. Now it's going to be just like before. All those papers he scattered all over the globe? I've got 'em. Now we just have to wait till you wake up and tell us where the last set is, and we're home free. Hey, I've got an idea. You know, we might even get out of this kidnapping charge? If she stays nuts, we can say we took her out to amuse her, that she told us to take her."

"What about the nurse? I hit her pretty hard."

"She'll do anything for the old lady. If I tell her that keeping shut will keep Eleanor alive, and that we'll let her stay with her when we send her off to the booby hatch, she'll go for it," he finished with certainty.

Alholm smiled. "So now we just get those papers, and we're clear on the murder rap." He laughed. "We could come out of this smelling like roses."

They laughed together and started to plan what they'd do next; maybe go down south and run a scam on some pre-Columbian art, just for the hell of it, just for the adventure of getting around the Federales, maybe knocking off a few nosy cops and peasants while they were at it. Ho ho, what a jolly good time they would have.

Consequently, they failed to realize that before she'd even been hustled into the van, Eleanor had come back to this world.

As previously recounted, the police had lost the van. So, glum-faced and clueless, Doan and Luke had slunk back to the apartment, now deserted, save for Binky.

"I am now going to have a much-needed cocktail,"

Doan announced, throwing his jacket on a chair. "Anyone care to join me?"

"Make it two," Binky added, collapsing on the sofa.

"Three," Luke finished, also landing on the sofa and putting his head in Binky's lap, whereupon she began to soothingly stroke his hair.

Doan handed out the cocktails and took the chair. "Good night, all," he said, taking one sip of his drink and sliding down in the chair. Then a moment later he was bolt upright. "Eleanor is perfectly safe."

"What?" Luke asked.

"The papers! The papers on Charles! They're scattered all over the globe. If he finds out we've already got the goods on him, he won't have any reason for holding Eleanor."

Luke hesitated before telling Doan, "Doan, if we already have the papers on him, that means she's useless to him—so he can kill her."

"That is a bit sticky," Doan confessed. "But, listen. Who do you think has done all the killing? Charles is not the kind of man who'd get his hands dirty. No, Alholm's the one who does the killing, I'll bet on it. Charles is evil, but deep in his heart, he's just a wimp. We have to separate them and make sure Eleanor ends up with Charles, not Alholm. Then, if we tell Charles we've already got the goods on him, he'll know the game is over. He'll give Eleanor up."

Luke mulled it over for a minute. "I think you're

right. But the question is, how do we split them up if we can't even find them?"

Doan smiled. "Ah, the power a cocktail has to restore one's mental faculties! Here's how. . . ."

Eleanor might have been old and ill, but she was not stupid. Until she could sort out the wealth of information she'd acquired in those few short minutes after coming back from France, she knew it was to her advantage to act as if she were still quite gone. Never has "La Marseillaise" been sung more stirringly or more off-key than it was sung in that van as it sped through Civic Center, nor had it often ended as suddenly as it did when they came to a screeching halt in front of the old neoclassical Museum of Modern Art on Van Ness, now abandoned for a new museum, a building that looks like Madonna's striped Hollywood mansion with a short stubby penis thrusting out of it. They escorted her to the front door, where she announced she was more than ready to meet the Nazi firing squads (Doan's filling her in on her periods of blankness was now proving invaluable) and demanded a last cigarette as her right under the Geneva Convention. She had no idea whether it was true or not, but it sounded good. Alholm produced a key and let them in, turning off the alarm. It seemed there was no corner of the art world where Alholm's arm did not reach.

They took her to a room whose sole objet d'art was a cage hanging from the ceiling, painted various colors. Much to her surprise, this turned out to be a working cage, for which Alholm had another key. She was shoved unceremoniously into it and the door was locked behind her.

"German pig!" she shouted at the retreating figures. "Now," she muttered to herself once they were gone, "what the hell do I do?"

Certain things were clear from the overheard conversation. First, that the cops were onto Charles for his art scams. Second, that murder was involved as well. Third, that the copies of her documentation on Charles's wrongdoings that Doan had deposited had somehow been recovered. So fourth, the set she had secreted in San Francisco was the only remaining one, and its existence was perhaps the only reason she was still alive. "Fifth, I am in it very, very deep."

Then she realized that perhaps worst of all, her would-be rescuers were operating under false assumptions. What measures would they take if they were confident they had the goods on Charles when they really didn't? As she realized that for the first time in her life she was truly helpless, she began to cry.

But that stopped quickly; she made it stop. She needed to be strong, but more than that, she needed to be sharp. Nothing could be allowed to interfere with her mental processes now, especially not anything like grief and self-pity that could send her back. "So I'm on my own. So be it. Now, think of something."

So she began to think, idly moving from side to side so that the cage began to move with a slight, hypnotic rhythm. Her body was useless, that was a fact, even if she could get free of this cage she was still too infirm to make a break for it or overpower anyone. Her mind, well, an incredible sharpness had been given her by God's grace, and that must be her tool. It would have to be something she could do from *in here*.

SIX

❧

Although Eleanor took all day formulating her plan, she had little trouble with the general scheme. Since Alholm was the only one she saw, as he brought her meals, he was the one she would have to work on. And what to say to a nut case like this one wasn't hard to think of, either. It was the particulars that had taken up most of her thoughts. Because the problem was first to concoct a story he would buy, but second and more important, to do it in such a way that she would not become the victim of whatever rage she drove him into.

"Dinner," he announced that second night, bringing her a Burger King bag. "Eat up."

She took the bag from him with a smile that unnerved him. "What's so funny?" he demanded.

She shrugged, hiding the smile behind her burger but not losing it.

179

"Hey," he said, reaching into the cage and grabbing her wrist. "What the hell's going on. Spill it right now, or you'll starve."

Then she laughed. "Oh, my poor Lieutenant, you are a child playing a man's game."

He ran his hands through his hair, jumping with nervous energy from one foot to the other. The Nazi bit was wearing on his nerves, but they were still street-smart nerves, and they told him the lady may be crazy, but right now she knew something he didn't. That was enough for him.

He took her dinner out of her hands. "Starve, then."

"That is a violation of the Geneva Convention! The Red Cross will hear about this!"

"Mmmm," he said, waving the burger just out of her reach. "Doesn't it smell good? Huh?" Then without warning he dropped it, grabbed her arm, pulled her forward, put his other arm through the cage and hit her in the face. She screamed in surprise more than in pain, although that came a split second later.

"Talk!"

She took her free hand off her face and looked up at him. "All right. It's all the same to me, now. And you're all the same. Why should I care what you and your Commandant do to each other?"

"What do you mean?" he growled, not letting go.

"I heard him on the phone. With someone in the Allies. He's planning his surrender, mein herr." What she *had* really heard was Charles telling Alholm that he was getting nervous, and that was enough to convince her this ruse would work.

He looked at her blindly for a moment, seeing with that survivor's instinct a dozen instant plans for escape. Then he came back to himself. "You're lying," he said in a flat tone.

"He was speaking to a Captain Fisher, Lieutenant," she said, using the name of Detective Faraglione's supervisor, which Doan had mentioned when he was telling her about the SoMa murders, and his suspicions about Charles. "Does this not sound like the name of an Allied officer to you?"

At that name, Alholm turned cold and knew she was telling the truth. He knew Fisher was Luke's boss. In fact, he knew quite a lot about the Police Department.

"Do you want to know the rest, Lieutenant?" she said, laughing freely now. "When the Allies take Paris, and you, he will go free and you will hang for your war crimes!"

Alholm let her go and left the room. Now what? he asked himself. Kill Charles, the strongest voice urged.

No, the cool voice contradicted. Remember, you have a source. Someone who can tell you if all this is true or not. Assume the worst, but hold off.

Charles was sitting at the table in the office kitchen. "I think it's time we moved again," he said to Alholm.

Alholm said nothing while he poured his coffee and weighed this. That would be his instructions from the cops, he thought. Because they won't just barge in here when they know we've . . . I've got the old lady. Eleanor, he decided, would live. Now that the cops were practically at the doors, he could use such a perfect hostage. Besides, when they knew where he was, he'd know they knew.

"Oh, yeah?" he finally said. "Where do you think we should take her?"

"I don't know. But I don't want to stay here more than another day."

"Sure. We'll think of a place tomorrow. Okay?"

Charles smiled, visibly relieved. "Good. Great. Okay."

Alholm smiled back.

"So anyway," Doan finished, "that's it."

The assembled audience was quiet. Finally Soheila whispered, "Wow."

The spell broken, everyone spoke at once. "Forget it, Doan," Binky said. "Stick to strategy."

Stan, protective arm around him, counseled, "Hey, come on, babe, I just got you back. This is too dangerous."

Doan looked to Luke. "Well?"

"No."

He realized one person hadn't spoken. He turned to KC. "And will you explain that smile for me? What's the matter? Never mind, I know. You think silly Doan has finally flipped out completely. Thinks he can be Nancy Drew. Never mind what you think, anyway."

"I think it's a great idea," KC said.

Doan's already distracted head whipped back around. *"What?!"*

"I think it's gutsy, it's smart, and it'll work."

Doan continued to stare at him. "Are you serious?"

KC nodded. "And if no one else will, I'll be your backup."

Doan started laughing. "God has a strange sense of humor. Luckily, he gave me one just like it. It would be an honor and a pleasure," he said with a regal bow, "to work with you." And then he turned to Luke.

"What you have just witnessed," he began, "is history. The most cautious, dare we say rabbity in his decision-making, person . . ." He turned to KC with a sweet smile. "No personal offense . . . has just agreed that this is a great plan. And can you think of anything else? Right now, with Eleanor in mortal danger?"

Luke rubbed his eyes. Neither he nor Doan had gotten more than a few hours of sleep since Eleanor had been taken, but Doan was still alert—more than alert—practically vibrant. And, right now, he was on the warpath with an idea stuck in his head, and that was a force hard to resist at full strength. Luke's reservations were only those of procedure. Endangering civilians was a no-no. But then he remembered the jimmied locks, the internal documents photocopied for Doan's staff by a club kid temporary, the degree of undoubtedly non-regulation involvement Doan already had.

"Besides, I don't need your permission. A private citizen is entitled to do anything that's not illegal—"

"All right. Fine. Whatever. I'll back you up."

Doan and KC simultaneously shouted a cheer, then stopped short and looked at each other, then blushed. "Well," Doan said, "I've got some preparing to do. So if you all would excuse me . . ."

There was a general movement to go. "KC," Doan said, tripping over it even as he realized that this was the first time he had pronounced those initials out loud, "could you stay a minute?"

"Sure."

The others left, Stan going out last after giving Doan a kiss and a squeeze and a "Later, babe."

Doan shut the door behind him and turned to face KC. "I can think of few things I hate more than being called *babe.*"

KC laughed. "You could tell him to stop."

"Yeah. But there are other things, too. I don't know. He was interesting when I met him. And need I say irresistible? But it's another case of my usual disease: great passion, yes; day-to-day compatibility, no. Like a drink?"

"Sure."

"Scotch?"

"How'd you know?"

"Guys like you always drink scotch." He made the drinks and they sat down in the living room again. "I just wanted to thank you for backing me up. I knew I could wear Luke down eventually, but you made it easy for me."

"Like I said, it sounds like a good plan. So, tomorrow you call Art Mill and this Chamberlain guy?"

"Oh, no," he said blithely. "That's all already taken care of."

KC laughed. "So you started the ball rolling, and then you told Luke? Why?"

"In case he said no, I mean really, absolutely, no, as in the Police Department will stop you no. Then I'd just tell him it is now ten P.M. and too late to stop the presses, so take it like a trooper and help me out. Of course, I was hoping he'd say okay. He'll be mad at me anyway, when he finds out I was going to do it no matter what."

"You can just exercise your not immodest charm and get him to write it off to basic Doan-type behavior."

Doan laughed and noticed KC's smile for the first time. What on earth makes me think I need someone exciting? Doan thought. I'm exciting enough for ten men, he said without immodesty. So he's dull. I could liven him up a little. And he could be my anchor . . . silly goose! he chided himself. You of all people should know those people always marry their own kind. He's just being friendly.

KC, meanwhile, was thinking how beautiful Doan looked in his peach dress.

Doan called Art early the next morning.

"Is it in there?"

"Of course it's in there," Art bristled. "Don't you read my column?"

"I don't get the paper, remember?"

"Oh, right. Ignorance is bliss."

"Exactly. I made that phrase up, did you know?"

"Aren't you supposed to be at Alholm's office?"

"KC's picking me up in a bit, but it's still early. Artists and thieves sleep till noon. How're things with you?"

Art laughed. "All hell broke loose this morning. The editor didn't know what was in my column until his wife read it to him at breakfast. Can you believe it? The editor doesn't read my column! I could have written about anything and gotten away with it. Get a load of this. He told me I had some nerve not turning hard news over to him! Like I'm supposed to stick to bubble gum. I was a real reporter back when he was—ah, never mind. What's past is past. At any rate, your little bomb is definitely having an effect. Anthony Chamberlain and I talked art for hours after we got the item written.

"You couldn't find a better husband."

"No doubt, if that's what I was in the market for. Now, you be careful today, Doan."

"I will. I have several knights in shining armor today, and you are not the least of them."

"Scoot. Call me when it's over."

"When it's over? You're a reporter, aren't you? Call Luke and demand to go with him so you can cover the arrest."

"You are absolutely right. Dammit, that's just what I'll do, and that goddamn editor can . . ."

The buzzer rang. "KC's here, I have to go."

"Right. Good luck!"

Steve Alholm was not thinking of escape routes at the moment. No animal instinct rose up to tell him which way to run. He was in the middle of the road, and the fast-approaching headlights were all he could see or think of.

The paper lay at his feet on the floor, Art Mill's column still in his sight.

Good morning, good morning. How are you all doing today? Better than fugitives from justice Steven Alholm and Charles Ambermere, I have no doubt. Not only are they wanted for kidnapping and murder, but it seems a sizable number of works in their collection have been declared forgeries. Anthony Chamberlain, art critic for the *San Francisco Times* as well as the S.F. Police Department's expert in the SoMa Killer case, has reviewed the collection and identified a number of the forgeries. Chamberlain is an expert on the works of Mortimer Arbuthnott, among others, and thinks that Alholm may have sold one genuine work by the artist, the rest forgeries. Alholm's angry customers filed a class action suit yesterday in U.S. District Court, calling for a seizure of Alholm's and Ambermere's assets in repayment. Judge Arthur Robinson issued an order freezing the assets of both defendants. In granting the order, Robinson cited the defendants' being fugitives from justice as the reason for his prompt action. So, should Alholm and Ambermere escape the country, they'll discover that they are the first case affected by the agreement with the Bahamian government signed last week regarding bank disclosure and asset seizure, and are consequently not just wanted but wanting.

Meanwhile, one San Franciscan artist is taking measures of his own. Stan Parks, falsely accused of being the SoMa Killer and freed only days ago from jail, is sending his representative, Doan McCandler, to the site of the Alholm/Ambermere lot today to comb through his works and weed out the forgeries. "Stan's prison time got him a lot of publicity," Mr. McCandler stated, "and consequently his works are increasing daily in value. We feel it is of the essence to guard his reputation against any further damaging rumor. It's going to be a long, lonely day tomorrow, but it's worth it."

"Son of a bitch," Alholm muttered. He'd forgotten about the money, he really had. There had been so much of it, it had just become something that would always be there, that he could always count on. Just because you killed someone, they couldn't take away your honestly earned proceeds. Just ask OJ! But this . . . now he had nothing. And that wasn't the worst of it. Forgeries? Was this guy crazy? The kind of money he was making on the genuine article, three daubs on a canvas for ten thousand bucks the last day he'd worked before this whole disaster, hell, he hadn't needed to forge anything.

Charles. Yes, that made sense. That stupid son of a bitch had really done it now. Goddamn his cowardly ass! No wonder the cops were willing to let him off, at least for the murders. With no money for a lawyer, Alholm was dead meat in court. They'd give him life for the kidnapping alone.

Charles came in and saw the look on his face. "What? What is it?"

Alholm threw him the paper. Charles read it, turning purple. "No."

"Yep. Broke. Because of you."

"What the hell are you talking about?"

"The forgeries, you asshole! You had to go and kill the golden goose. God, you are so stupid!"

"I swear to God, I don't know anything about any forgeries! I don't! There aren't any, this is a lie. . . . Wait. Wait."

"What?"

"McCandler. This guy who's going to be at the gallery. That's the faggot. The one she sent around the world with the papers."

"So?"

Charles smiled. "Do you want Eleanor to talk or not?"

"No games, you hear me? Spit it out."

"He'll be there all alone. We'll get him. And if you don't think seeing him getting cut to pieces before her eyes will get her to talk, well—"

"She's nuts, she can't tell us anything."

"Shock sent her into it, right?"

Alholm considered. Was this the trap, then, that Captain Fisher had ready to spring on him? Or did this new development mean the deal was off? That would be like Charles, too, to change sides when the wind changed. Especially if he had just realized what Alholm had about his fate in the hands of the police, now that he was an ordinary impoverished citizen who'd seriously broken the law. Instinct told him Charles had the right idea.

"All right. I'll go get him. You get her ready to travel. I'll call you and tell you where to go."

Doan was completely calm. Logic was his perfect shining weapon this morning. If Charles and Alholm ransacked the house before taking Eleanor, it was because they needed the last set of papers. If they took Eleanor, it was because they didn't find them and needed her to tell them where those papers were. If Eleanor was still their living captive a day later, it meant she hadn't told them yet. If she shouted "Vive la Revolution" from a speeding van, it meant that she'd slipped and was not likely to be able to tell them where those papers were. That slip back into fantasyland had bought Doan valuable time. He knew that she had to be back by now; but still not talking. They would want a lever to use on her. She was a tough old girl, he knew. Physical violence short of torture would not move her. Charles knew what Doan meant to Eleanor. Doan was now known to them to be alone and unguarded today. Thus, the lever had offered itself.

Alholm would come for him, he was sure. He could not afford not to. There was only one problem. Alholm's office was a converted loft, and consequently there was nowhere to hide the requisite backup policemen (handpicked by Luke for their trustworthiness and discretion). Said cops would have to stay out of sight until called upon at the crucial moment. Luke and Doan were to be the only ones inside the building.

"Coffee?" Luke asked, proferring a thermos.

"I have to pee badly enough already."

"So go."

"The bathrooms are locked."

Luke held up his hand for silence. "I heard a car."

His walkie-talkie clicked twice, confirming his hearing, but then clicked twice more, indicating Alholm was not alone.

They looked at each other. "He wouldn't bring Eleanor. . . ." Luke supposed.

"He would."

Luke ducked into his appointed hiding place in the office; Doan jumped up with his clipboard and stood in front of a canvas, making notes.

The door to the loft opened. There were two sets of

footsteps, all right, but they were both rapid and strong. "Good morning, good morning! I'm just about done here," Doan said, turning around. "If you'll just—oh my God," he said, his shock genuine.

Luke stood up. "Police! Don't—" and lost the policeman's only advantage, the one second of surprise, when he saw the face of the man with Alholm. Alholm raised a silencer-equipped pistol and shot Luke in the chest. He fell with a grunt and passed out from the pain.

"Now then," Alholm said with a smile. "To business. Good morning, good morning, yourself, you clever little bastard."

"There's nowhere you can hide now. You're broke."

Alholm laughed. "You liar. There wasn't any seizure. At least, all that money I've got in the Bahamas is just fine. And now I'm going to go claim it."

"The cops are outside."

"Oh, I know. But we have a hostage now, don't we? It was really too easy. Two clicks meant I was here, two more meant I wasn't alone. Detective Faraglione wasn't very thorough on that point, was he? Two more clicks just meant I could be with anyone. As you see. There's nothing I can do to the police to get them off my back, except . . . well, as you see, discover their every move in advance."

"We already have Charles in custody. What's in those papers will put you both in the chair. There's more than one set, you know. There's—"

"Five, total."

Alholm's companion came forward. "Five sets. And I'll be thankin' ye for the fine vacation I had. Hah! Crazy cousin Doan, into Mother's closet again, and her safe, too! We just let him go his way, pulling his stunts. Mother prefers it that way, and Mother holds the purse strings. But here's a letter from her, my good man, so would you return those papers to me, please? Ah, too easy," Sergeant Seamus Flaharity said with a sigh. "Just like candy from a baby."

"Every set. We got every set but hers. And you're going to help us get them out of her."

"He's crazy," Doan couldn't help but say to Flaharity, "so he has some kind of excuse. You're just a bug."

Flaharity flushed. "I'll show you a thing or two—"

"Hold on. If you want to beat him up, go ahead. But give me the gun. We need him alive."

Flaharity handed the gun to Alholm and advanced on Doan.

Two things happened at once. A foot left the floor and landed in Flaharity's crotch with a speed that amazed. A figure jumped from the rafters and landed squarely on top of Alholm, smashing him to the floor.

Flaharity screamed and doubled over. Doan picked up a canvas and drove the corner of the frame into the back of Flaharity's neck.

Alholm still struggled with his attacker, each of them with a hand on the gun. Doan jumped to where Luke lay and seized his gun, pointing it at the two combatants, too unsure to fire. Then Alholm threw the man into Doan; the two of them collapsed in a heap. Only then did Doan realize that it was KC who had saved his life.

"Kiss me," Doan demanded, and KC did just that.

Luke was awake when they packed him into the ambulance; his bulletproof vest had shielded him from serious harm. "Alholm?" he asked Doan.

"Under arrest, darling, thanks to you."

"Doan, listen: Don't tell Binky I got shot in the chest. She'll think it's worse than it is."

"I'll make it sound positively awful," Doan promised. "As if you're hovering near death's doorstep."

"Oh, no, please, you'll scare her."

"Don't you want that girl to make up her mind once and for all that you are the man for her?"

"Yeah, but—"

"No buts. Off you go!" he said, cheerily slamming the ambulance door. "Now," he said to KC, "to save Eleanor."

The phone had assumed the persona of all the fates to Charles. Alholm had been gone three hours! There was something wrong.

"Lunch!" Eleanor shouted for the fifth time in as many minutes.

"Shut up!"

"Lunch lunch lunch lunch lunch lunch lunch lunch!"

Charles stormed into the back room. "I swear to God, I'm going to kill you."

"Do it, pig! Add it to your war crimes!"

"Where the hell is he?" he muttered to himself.

"What?"

"None of your business."

"The other one? You mean you don't know?"

"Know what?"

"Oh, he's gone for good."

"No. You don't know that."

"Sure I do. He told me."

"*No!*" he screamed. "What did he say?"

"Lunch lunch lunch lunch!"

He bellowed and ran to the cage, fumbled with the keys, opened the door, and tore her out of it, throwing her to the floor. *"What did he say!"*

"Ow, stop! You're hurting me! I'll tell you! He found the last set of papers. And decided to take all the money for himself."

"There is no money."

"There was another account. In Paraguay. Where all good Nazis keep their accounts," she added for good measure. She hoped his fear would prevent him from noticing how casually she'd mentioned the papers, but she'd had to slip character to play that card, no matter how dangerous it might be.

"Oh my God, I'm doomed. Doomed!" He cradled his head in his arms for a moment, sobbing. Then he looked up with murder in his eyes. "And it's all your fault, you bitch. If you'd kept to your bed like a good girl, none of this would have happened. But you had to run around and be a fool with that faggot, and go crazy. Worst of all, you had to get better. So I'm going to jail, so what?" he said with a casualness that chilled her. "First I'm going to do what I've always wanted to do. I'm going to kill you."

Some of Alholm's insanity had reached Charles. But even as his hands began to close around her throat, she looked at him with steel in her eyes and said, "You need a hostage."

It worked. An option, a way out, was enough to bring back the real Charles, the chicken. Indecision met murder and stopped it cold. He turned around and began wringing his hands.

That was all she needed. She seized the cage and pushed it as hard as she could, then hit the deck. The force it picked up on its way back was not great, but it was enough to knock Charles off his feet when it hit him square in the back, and that was all she asked.

"Oof!" was all he said as he hit the floor facefirst.

Eleanor rolled out of the cage's path, got up, and ran.

The alarms were going full blast at the museum when Doan, KC, and a small army of policemen arrived. "They're gone," Doan decided instantly. "Eleanor got away from him, at least momentarily, and got out through one of those Alarm Will Sound doors. Sweep the area," he commanded the policeman driving their car. "We'll find her."

• • •

The day Eleanor had been kidnapped was a day like any other. Which meant that her MUNI Fast Pass was tucked securely in her blouse, along with a BART ticket. Should the urge to go off and explore hit her (as it often had since her recovery) at any time, she was ready. She was so happy to just be able to walk out the door and go wherever she wanted, under her own power. For all her wealth, it was this little thing that made Eleanor Van Owens happiest.

And as a frequent rider of the city's public transportation, she knew that the Van Ness subway station was only blocks away. She couldn't outrun Charles, she had no money for a cab (it didn't occur to the poor dear to flag one down and beg for help), and (this did make sense) if there was one thing she knew that Charles didn't, it was public transit.

By the time Charles woke up and began his pursuit, she was almost at the station. Unfortunately, he wasn't entirely stupid. He was aware of his wife's habits, and made a beeline for that same destination.

The police cruiser circled around the area. "Nothing," Doan wailed.

KC clasped his hand. "Soon."

A pedestrian flagged the cruiser down. "Hey, I don't know if it means anything, but I saw an old lady run down into the station looking real scared, and this real mean-looking guy just ran down there, too. I think he's after her."

"Eleanor!" Doan shouted, jumping out of the car. KC and the police officer were right behind him.

Eleanor knew it didn't matter which train you got on when you were going downtown from here; they all went straight down Market Street and dead-ended at the Embarcadero station. The train was just pulling into the station when she saw Charles.

She hid on the other side of the escalator and hoped she could get on the train before he saw her. In vain.

She felt a breeze, even though the train had come to a stop. The way forest dwellers can tell on the wind what animal approaches, so the city dweller can tell from that underground breeze that another train is coming into the station from the opposite direction.

She dashed into the downtown-bound train, waiting to hear the bell ring that would announce the doors were closing. Charles made it through the doors into the next car up.

She looked at the sign that was now flashing to announce the destination of the train coming from downtown. Two car train, one J car, one N car. She had a brainstorm just as the bell started ringing. She was out the doors of the car just as they closed.

Charles forced his bulk between the doors of his car, causing them to reopen, and went after her.

She ran for her life, probably faster than she'd ever run before, and prayed to God that she wouldn't trip.

She made it into the N car. Charles made it into the J car. The doors shut.

And she laughed.

Charles cursed, first silently, then loudly. Why the hell was this train moving so slow? He guessed it couldn't be doing more than ten miles an hour.

Relax, he told himself. Just think of her in the next car, as scared as a mouse is when you hold it in your hand. She knows what's coming.

The train lurched as it changed tracks and began to come up out of the ground. It stopped when it reached the street. There was a shudder and a rumble. Charles looked out the window. The car ahead had detached, and his was turning down Church Street!

Eleanor had taken a window seat so as to smile and wave prettily at Charles as the subway car, now streetcar, rolled away.

"I hate you!" he shouted. "I hate you! and I'll *get you yet!*"

SEVEN

❧

ELEANOR'S RESCUE EFFECTED, DOAN LOST INTEREST IN THE case almost immediately. "After all," he reasoned to Eleanor, "Charles still has some money squirreled away, so he's probably left the country, anyway. Besides, it really wouldn't do us any good to catch him, since he'd just hire good lawyers and get off." They were sitting in her living room, having tea served by a more-than-usually-solicitous Frannie.

"Doan!" Eleanor chided him, clinking her fine china cup into its saucer. "That's awfully cynical."

He eyed her levelly. "I have three words for you, dearie: Claus Von Bulow."

"Mmm. Well, at least Flaharity and Alholm are behind bars now." She paused to take a very unladylike swallow. "Listen, I've had this fabulous idea. I want to throw a party next Saturday night; not too many people—"

201

"Saturday? Darling, if you're going to have a party next Saturday, it's going to have to be *huge*, or nobody will come at all."

"Why ever not?"

Why ever not, indeed! any gay San Franciscan would sniff. A little background: the gay season in San Francisco is not mandated like that of other resort villages around the heterosexual calendar, which opens the festivities on Memorial Day and closes them on Labor Day. San Francisco's season opens on the last Sunday in June, with the Gay Pride Parade, and ends four months later, after the Folsom, Castro, and Dore Alley street fairs, on the coming Saturday night on which Eleanor had planned her party: October 31, aka Halloween, the highest of homo holy days, the gay Saturnalia, four blocks of Babylon, *two hundred and fifty thousand homosexuals,* all in costume and most in drag.

Each year the event, which closes off most of the Castro District's streets, is beseiged with a multitude of heterosexual gawkers who come in from the far provinces across the bay to see the queers at play, and occasionally beat them up, too. And each year, many grumble that the whole thing should just be moved to Folsom Street one year, and not tell *them,* so that they all come to the Castro only to see each other, resplendently authentic in their yahoo costumes. But it never happens; after all, homosexuals are tolerated so well in San Francisco because they are one of the tourist attractions. The heterosexual citizens could no more risk alienating them than they would dare to blow up Alcatraz. So we, in turn, continue to do our bit for the tourist industry, holding hands in public, dressing up on Halloween, and all the other shocking appurtenances of gay life, and the festival proceeds apace.

Those who truly cannot stand the frenzy of the actual Halloween night plunk down their hard-earned money for a ticket to the Muscle Sisters Ball, an affair generally held in the Castro the weekend before H Day. The rest of us put up with the madness in the hope that our one-night illusion, above all others, will be the one remembered for years to come.

For Doan, this meant one night a year on which it could be said, without his being able to deny it, that he did drag. Of course, being Doan, he didn't just do drag. He'd done that his first year in the city, when he'd gone out in full regal splendor as Marie Antoinette, only to discover, to his horror, six other doomed queens in the same outfit, all of whom completed his mortification by shouting, "Off with his head!" at their first sight of him. Doan had made his first—and last—bumpkin's mistake, which can generally be summarized as doing the first clever thing that comes to mind without stopping to wonder if anyone else has been equally clever in the past. (This particular year, the bumpkin's mistake would be to think you and your best friend were the only homosexuals in town who'd thought to dress as Patsy and Edina.)

As his savvy and social circle increased, so did the scale of Doan's Halloween enterprises. The previous year, he'd staged a Medici Family Reunion (at eight o'clock, repeated at ten, twelve, and two) in the middle of Market Street, which ended with all participants theatrically splayed across the pavement in dramatically dead poses. His plans for this year's effort was a closely guarded secret, even from Binky.

"I know it's going to be something imperial," she sighed airily. "Last year you almost got poisoned for real because you wouldn't let anyone else be Catherine di Medici."

Doan did not, for once, rise to the bait. The secret was too delicious to be extracted by mere taunts. "Of course it will be something imperial," he sniffed, "but that certainly leaves the field wide open. I could be Catherine the Great, riding a pillow to ecstasy, or Elizabeth II—who wouldn't pay me to see the contents of my purse? Or Lady Jane Grey, Queen for a Day—"

"Never mind," she sighed. "I suppose I'll just have to be *surprised*," she spoke the last word scornfully.

"And what about you, dear? Who will manifest through you?"

"Well, if you're not telling, I'm not either. Suffice it to say I tend to go for a much more minimalist look than you do."

"Mmm. Listen, I need to borrow your drapes."

"I beg your pardon?"

"I need to borrow your drapes. You can have them back Sunday."

"Oh right, I'm going to loan my gauzy linen drapes to you in perfect shape and you're going to return them in the form of skimpy little dresses. I don't think so."

"They will be returned *intact*. I guarantee it."

She loaned him the drapes. What are friends for? She offered to meet him at a neutral place the morning of the big day for champagne and pastry, so that neither of them would have to resist the urge to paw through the other's closet looking for clues. But Doan pooh-poohed this, telling her to come to his place. This was not because he trusted her—he did not—but because his little thing required a much larger staging area than merely his apartment.

"Well, if we can't talk about tonight," she said, "we might as well talk about men."

"The men! I forgot all about them. What are you doing with yours tonight?"

"Luke's back to work already, and he's working the Castro tonight, on the beat. They need all the help they can get. Which is fine by me, because that gives me someone to hang out with and talk to until you deign to make your majestic entrance. It is safe to assume that your new love is shaving his moustache, even as we speak, for his role in tonight's comedy?"

Doan's new love, in fact, was KC. Never mind that

he had much more in common with Stan, or that the artist would as lief try to change Doan as he would try to make the world turn backward (which could not be said of KC). Nature has its own imperatives, even with those who might be considered among nature's closed circuits. If someone saves your life, why, you almost can't help it when your affections are transferred to that (otherwise highly inappropriate) person. And needless to say, opposites usually attract because the sex is *great*.

"He is not shaving, no. I will tell you that he is a participant. Really, Binky, you keep steering the conversation back to tonight!"

"All right, all right, I'll shut up." She disgruntledly shoveled a mini lemon tart into her mouth and washed it down with Veuve Clicquot. "Just tell me where and when to meet you tonight."

Doan smiled. "You won't be able to miss me."

Let it be said politely, first: Unless one is extremely gregarious, being crammed into a four block area, even if that area consists of generously spaced boulevards, with two hundred and fifty thousand strangers, is not a picnic. "Trick or treat!" a man in a raincoat and a John Bobbitt mask shouted at Binky, opening said coat to reveal a sign hung over his privates that said, "Please give generously." While under other circumstances, she might have been forced to smile tightly and politely, her character tonight enabled her to focus all her laserlike disgust at the man, who promptly shriveled up and died.

That done, she shifted her basket from one forearm to the other and made her way through the crowd. She'd made a late start, knowing that Doan would wait until at least midnight to show up to ensure maximum bang for his buck, and having been warned beforehand by Luke that he would more likely have his hands full with puking louts than he'd have free time to schmooze with her.

The streets held the usual collection of generic drag queens, most of them men who would shave their facial hair and don a dress this day and no other, including some sad souls in full boobs and tits extravaganza who wouldn't even part with their beards for the night; more than one of that beloved infidel of all oppressed peoples, Bart Simpson; and the legendary guy with the head, a man who wore his self-sculpted gigantic papier-mâché head of Madonna at all the gay season's grander street events.

It took her longer than usual to find Luke. While her six-four beau would have been literally head and shoulders above most crowds, the sheer height and scale of the artificial hairdos on display tonight conspired to conceal him from her view. When she did find him, he was trapped between a contingent of Radical Faeries on one side and Sisters of Perpetual Indulgence on the other. What had begun as a good-natured and completely unserious argument between the pagans and the nuns had somehow devolved into a shouting and shoving match, provoked by an inopportune faerie high heel pinning down the hem of a sister's habit. Binky waited a safe distance away as Luke played music to soothe the savage beasts (it didn't hurt the cause of peace that the peacemaker was so easy on the eyes, either).

"Your Nobel Prize is in the mail," she said.

Luke turned around to see her and lit up. "Hey!" Then a puzzled look crossed his face. "Who are you supposed to be?"

It was not a costume that your average straight man could figure out. Binky had cut her hair into a short do, had it dyed blond with intentionally distinct dark roots. Her clothes were expensive but nondescript: a pair of slacks and a white sweater. On her arm was a basket loaded with potpourri, little cookies artfully tied up in muslin bags, a few gardening implements, and a handful of charge cards.

"It's a secret," she said. "If you really want to know who I'm supposed to be, help me find Doan. He'll know right away; he'll tell you."

"All right. But I have to let the other guys know I'm temporarily deserting my post."

Binky waited impatiently for Luke's return, jostled constantly as she was by the press of the crowd. Then, just for a moment, she saw a face she recognized—a face so thoroughly plastered over the front pages of the local newspapers that even one as ignorant as she of current events could not have missed it: the face of Charles Ambermere. She blinked, and he was gone.

Was it really him? she wondered. She wouldn't put it past some queen to dress up as the city's latest celebrity murderer, but then again, she had never actually seen Ambermere herself, face to face. She thought it would be a good time for Luke to return—just in case.

But her efforts to locate him in the crowd were ended by a blast of four trumpets blown by scantily clad youths mimicking imperial pages. All movement came to a standstill as the crowd turned to see what was coming off of Sanchez and onto Market. Preadolescent drummers followed the trumpeters, then hunky legionnaires carrying the eagles of their legions. Then came the princesses—among the few authentic females on the whole street—scattering rose petals.

And then, around the corner, came the coup de grace: a splendid palanquin hoisted and carried by six shirtless beefcakes, most of whom were famous local porn stars and one of whom, Binky noted, was KC And of course, who should be the one carried on said palanquin, Binky's own gauze curtains pulled back to reveal him: Doan, his hair done in curly Roman ringlets, his eyes thick with dark makeup, his plain white toga neatly accessorized with a sash of the imperial purple, a laurel wreath on his head.

"I am your *empress,*" Doan shouted in a tone of voice that brooked no dissent. "Bow down before me!" Many actually did; others simply fell down trying to get out of the imperially rude majesty's way.

"Doan!" Binky shouted, pushing her way through

the cheering crowd, all of whom loved a spectacle. "Doan!"

"She may approach us!" Doan commanded the legionaries, who promptly shoveled multiple innocent bystanders out of the way to allow Binky through.

"Do you love it?" he whispered conspiratorially. "Have I outdone myself?"

"Doan, I just saw Charles Ambermere."

"Of course you did. I just saw Charles Manson! Who are you supposed to be, anyway?"

"No, I don't mean that. I mean the *real* Ambermere! Or at least I think it was. . . ."

"Don't be silly. What would he be doing here?"

"Coming to get revenge on you, I imagine."

Doan opened a fan with a snap—the fan was admittedly an anachronistic touch, but an effectively royal one, nonetheless—and snorted. "There are too many homosexuals here for Charles Ambermere to stand it. Besides, this is way too public a place for revenge." Noting that Binky was not appeased, he tried another tack. "Look. I'm doing a repeat performance of this entrance at Eleanor's party; I've got a chartered bus waiting to take me and all my supporting cast to her house. We won't loiter here long, all right? Just long enough for everybody to take pictures. Okay?" he said hurriedly, seeing the photographer from the *San Francisco Times* approaching.

Doan made a motion, and his palanquin was lifted above the heads of the throng. "My people!" Doan shouted, showering the populace with gold coins (actually a combination of gold foil-wrapped chocolates and Gold Coin condoms). Binky, accepting that stardom trumped safety every time, sighed and made her way to Doan's caravan of buses.

Eleanor's house blazed with light; every room was packed with people. Art Mill mingled with the skill gained from God knew how many decades of mingling; Anthony Chamberlain held Eleanor captive with explications on modern art; former inmate (and now artist *du jour*) Stan Parks was there with several aged men competing to be his benefactor. He and Doan had parted amicably, both recognizing a fling for what it was; moreover, Stan was a believer neither in holding a grudge nor in letting the grass grow under his feet. This was his moment in the media sun, and he was damned if he would let it pass by. Luke escorted Captain Fisher, having been pulled off Castro duty to do this honor.

Binky left Cecelia B. DeMille and her cast of thousands around the corner and quickly took refuge from the autumn chill in Eleanor's house. She spied Luke by a huge floral arrangement, grinning wickedly.

"What's so funny?" she asked.

"I just thought I'd stand here and see if I waited long enough, if you'd get your head stuck in here, and I could do the honors of pulling you out."

"Ha ha. Where's your costume?"

"I'm dressed as a policeman. Every gay man's fantasy, right? What better outfit for Halloween in San Francisco? You could introduce me around as your pet cop."

"I don't think I know many of these people. They're all friends of Eleanor and Doan."

"Well, then, introduce yourself. You call yourself a socialite?"

"I *never* called myself a socialite," Binky replied frostily. "Are you going to be gallant and get me a drink, or just stand here making fun of me?"

"Your wish is my command."

"My command is champagne."

Luke bowed low and deep and went in search of Binky's refreshment. Meanwhile, Binky decided to explore one of San Francisco's most eminent piles. Not being a big fan of large crowds, and having not only pushed her way through the throngs in the Castro, and also having been sat on in Doan's overcrowded bus by several giggling page boys, Binky was not thrilled about once more pushing her way through still throngier throngs in Eleanor's house. Her original intent of exploration was soon subsumed by her desire for a room of her own, if only for a few recuperative moments.

She soon found that her only option for such rest was to find a bathroom, but there were lines for those. Salvation came in the form of Eleanor, who recognized her as Doan's friend and pulled her out of line. "Upstairs, there's a locked door. It's my own private bathroom." She pressed a key into Binky's hands. "Help yourself."

"Thank you," Binky uttered with more feeling than she had ever given to those words before. She stole up the stairs to Eleanor's secret potty.

She had no sooner shut and locked the door than she was grabbed from behind. A strong, foul-smelling hand clamped over her mouth while the other twisted her arm behind her back. "Shit!" a voice said. Although she couldn't actually see him, she had no doubt who her assailant was: Charles Ambermere, who had realized it was not his intended victim he'd accosted but a stranger. "Well, I can make use of you anyway. I'm going to uncover your mouth, but you're not to make a sound, you hear?" he added.

Later she thought it a half mad thought, but Binky was desperate to ask him if he'd been in the Castro earlier, but didn't dare. Charles opened the door and maneuvered her in front of him. Binky thought fast, trying to fight through her panic to come up with some idea. "You can't go out that way," she said, indicating the main stairs. "There are too many people."

"And why are you being so helpful?" he sneered, pushing her toward the stairs.

From below she heard a gasp, then a cry of "Hey, watch it!" In a second she knew what to do. When the trumpets blared downstairs, announcing the arrival of the Empress Theodosia, Charles jumped in his skin, Binky reached into her basket, pulled out the gardening shears, and stabbed Charles's hand. Then she whipped around as he howled, holding his hand, and kicked him in the privates, then, after he bent over double, she dropped the shears, grabbed his shirt collar with both hands, and threw him headlong down the stairs. Charles tumbled again and again, the sound drowned out by the imperial procession. He lay at the bottom of the stairs, his head at an unnatural angle, and Binky sat down on the steps and began to sob.

Below her, Luke, a glass of champagne in hand, turned instantly from suitor to cop. "Quiet, everybody. Move back. There's been an accident." Luke calmed the panicked guests. He sent someone to find Captain Fisher.

Another guest approached the bottom of the stairs. "Eleanor's hairdresser said he and his boyfriend were coming as the killers from *In Cold Blood*. Maybe he meant *after* the hanging."

"Binky?" Luke said, hearing the sobbing from above. "Is that you?" Binky sobbed acknowedgment. He raced up the stairs two at a time. "What happened?"

"Ambermere," she sputtered. "Abduction. Nuts. Stairs." With Luke's help, she shakily descended.

Doan, eager to kill the person who had upstaged his entrance, was not displeased to find that somebody had already done the killing for him. Then he started. "Why, that's Charles Ambermere! What's he doing here?"

"From what I can tell," Luke said, "he was here to kidnap Binky."

"That doesn't sound right. He doesn't even know who she is."

"No!" Binky said, now feeling up to managing more complete sentences. "He was hiding in Eleanor's private bathroom, waiting for her to come in. Then he was going to . . . I feel faint." She felt entirely too close to the late Charles Ambermere.

"Oh my god, you're *Martha Stewart!*" Doan screamed. "You're Martha Stewart, deranged murderess! I love it!"

Binky's eyes rolled up in her head; Luke and Doan caught her just in time.

"Let's get her out of here, get her some fresh air," Doan suggested.

"Air," she agreed. "Drink. Must have cocktail."

Luke protested, but while his attention was taken by Captain Fisher, Doan whisked Binky through the crowd. "Coming through!" he shouted, elbowing his way to the bar. "She's very ill; she needs water to take her pills. Two Tanqueray martinis," he commanded when he finally make it to the bar, ignoring the glares of those he'd pushed aside. "Here you go, dear—liquid sedative." They retreated to the quietest corner they could find.

They both tossed their cocktails back and Doan nabbed two more from a passing tray. "Well, at least that's the end of Charles," Binky said. "Did he even know who I was? He seemed to—"

"He must have seen you earlier with Luke, eh?"

She shuddered. "God. Dating a policeman may be more dangerous than being one."

"Well, Martha, your Connecticut estate will never lack for excitement again."

"And just yesterday I thought that finally knowing what KC stood for would be the thrill of the week."

"*No!* He told you? He still won't tell me."

"I'm surprised you didn't go through his drawers, looking for bills and checks with his name on them."

"Of course I did. That is, I tried, but he keeps all his papers locked up—surely just to spite me."

"I'll tell you, on one condition."

"Name it, and then we'll see."

"You tell me how you got a name like Doan."

Doan laughed. "My mother is a woman with a sense of humor. To say the least. Carrying me put a strain on her back so bad she was in screaming pain for nine months. Suffice it to say the result is that I am an only child. When the little beast was finally out, to quote directly, she thought it was all over, but no! She had to think of a name. Percy, one aunt suggested. Cecil, said the next. Not for mother, thank you. No, she chose the one name that had been with her for nine months, a name that every time she called it would remind her never to do this again, the name on the bottle of pills that never left her sight."

Binky started laughing and was soon unable to stop. "And if you *ever* tell *anyone,* especially KC, I shall have your head," he concluded. "Really, with a name like Binky, you should talk!"

"And one day, Doan, I'll let *you* know how I got *my* name."

"Tell me now!"

"No. Maybe at the end of our next adventure, should we again be so discomposed by events."

Just then, what seemed like an entire battalion of San Francisco police burst into the party. Binky knew the press would not be far behind. "You know, life will never be this exciting again. There are no second acts in American lives, etc., etc."

Doan drained his martini and signaled for two more. "So true, darling, but you forget: In America, there may be no second acts, but there's no limit on *sequels!*"